A City of Ghosts

A City of Ghosts

by Betsy Phillips

For Bart

AUTHOR'S NOTE

None of the stories in this book are true.

These stories, I hope, have enough basis in fact that, if you find yourself in the locations in which they seem to take place, you might be tempted to squint and see if you can align the Nashville you know with the city in these tales.

If you do, you'll find the match isn't perfect.

The city of legends is often a very different place from the city on the map.

Both are real enough.

Table of Contents

October

A City of Ghosts

April

April 1ˢᵗ

THE INFAMOUS WITCH

A song sung in Tennessee often has two meanings—
one apparent to anyone who might hear it, and one coded
for a deliberate audience. You probably learned about this in
school, how a field full of people picking cotton might sing
"Follow the Drinking Gourd" to direct a man hidden in the
stand of trees to go north in the direction the Big Dipper
points, while the overseer sits on his horse, oblivious, but
enjoying the music.

That's the way the story of the witch goes, too. Some
folks tell the story as if it's a story about an old woman
angry about being cheated in a slave trade. Others tell it as
if it's a story about a man who couldn't keep his hands off his
daughter, and the embodiment of her unspoken fury.

It is a story about revenge, at least the way I heard it;
that much is true.

And it is a story of a young mother, but not the Bell
woman. This is the story of a young mother sold to a new
family, away from her babies, who swore to always hate the
whole family, to destroy them all, starting with the father—
the worst, the one with the sharp tongue and the quick fist.
But those were strange times, and eventually she softened
towards the women. Helped keep them safe, as she could, as
safe as she could.

She could wander around the house unnoticed. She
knew what plants in the wilds of Robertson County could
kill. She could slip the poison into the food. She could work
the foot magic that hobbled the old man. She could speak
without anyone noticing her mouth moving. She could make
an animal do her bidding. She could stop a president in his
tracks. And she could read, though no one knew that but
her.

"Do you know Marie Laveau?"

"Yes," I said.

"This woman could have been like that, if she wasn't stuck out in the country. If you know the Work, you can recognize a Worker. And the Witch was a powerful Worker. You hear that story, if you know what to listen for, and you hear the story of the greatest hoodoo woman in Tennessee. Hands down."

"Do you think she still haunts that place?"

"Sure I do."

"Have you seen her?"

"Oh, no. I don't mess with things that powerful. Now my grandmother, in her day, she might have. She was fearless. But not me. I know better. There's trouble."

"Why do you think she's still there?"

"Because that's her land, now, sweetie. That's the point of the story—you do the Work, you get the reward."

April 2ⁿᵈ

THE MAN IN MY BACK YARD

My house sits on an acre of land in Whites Creek, just north of Nashville, still sort of Nashville. The houses on my side of the road are all 1950s ranch houses with two bedrooms, one bath. All the same layout, though some have full porches and some have fireplaces and some are mirror images of their neighbors. And over half a century, they have come to take on their own personalities, with additions and coats of paint and the deaths of the people who first owned them.

I bought my house from the nephew of the original owners. His aunt is still alive. His uncle has been dead a while, but his shed in the back yard still has his small animal traps, rusted, but hanging on the wall. His work bench still has drill bits and chisels. The cabinet above the sink still had his two white glass mugs. And I found jars of honey in there from when he used to keep bees.

The nephew told me that toward the end of his life, his uncle went blind. So they draped ropes and wires all around the backyard so the uncle could still get outside and walk around and, following the ropes, not get lost. Because he didn't want to be cooped up in the house. He wanted to be out in the yard that he loved so much.

Often, when people come to visit, they come in the back door and they ask, "Is that your dad out in the hammock?"

And I say, "No. There's no one here but me."

But I hope I'm wrong.

April 3rd

WHERE IT USED TO BE

Nashville is starting to look more and more like a movie set, like somebody who's never been to a city's idea of what a city should look like—all too-perfect new glass buildings and color-coordinated condominiums of rose brick and sand concrete.

Still, the citizens refuse to succumb completely to a landscape the past can't stick to. And so, when you are given directions to anywhere, they are full of the haunts of Nashville's past. If you, for instance, are trying to get from the bus station, which by the time you read this will probably be torn down, which makes this such a Nashville story— getting rid of things to make room for things we will soon enough get rid of ...

Where was I? Oh, yes.

Say you wanted to get from where the bus station used to be, there on Eighth Avenue, to the children's hospital. Well, you'd as likely as not be told to go up by where the Hall of Fame used to be and then down Division past where Patrick's was and when you get to where Nick & Rudy's was, across from where the IHOP used to be, turn left and go past where the Burger King was, and soon enough, you'll see it on your right.

It seems like Nashville is in a constant hurry to get rid of everything that ties it to its own history. But if you know where to look and how to listen, the ghosts are all around us.

April 4ᵗʰ

THE HOUSE ON SIGLER STREET

Weirdly enough, I was with my Mom at the Melrose Kroger and she was telling me about her friend, Helen, who had just been in the house on Sigler Street after having bought it, and how Helen said there was nothing, absolutely nothing, wrong with it, when the woman in line in front of us started to shake and spilled her purse all over the floor.

Her face was drawn. I scrambled to get her things back in her purse while my mom put her arm around the woman and tried to keep her upright.

"Y'all talking about that house at the end of Sigler Street?" She gave us the house number and my mom said, "Yes, that's the one."

"I used to live there," she said. "We rented that place."

"So, is it true?" I asked.

"Yes," she said, so firmly that I felt bad that my mom and I had been having such good fun laughing about it. She went on. "That lady's stuff was still in the house. Not all of it. But there was a big chest, like a foot locker, that we never could get in, that was in the bedroom. And one of the closets had a bunch of her old dresses. And you'd just find shit ... stuff, I mean ... all the time. Like, you'd go to get a spoon out of the drawer and there'd be a lacy handkerchief in there. Old-fashioned. Looked handmade. Not there before and not mine. That's for sure.

"We'd hear someone walking around the house all the time. And we had a cat and it would never go in the bathroom. You don't want a cat in the bathroom, but it would sit, for hours, and just stare into the bathroom, but it never, ever went in there.

"That place is wrong. There's something wrong with it.

"Your friend should not live there."

Well, we thought the conversation was strange, but we didn't bother to mention it to Helen, because she wasn't going to live there, she was just going to rent it out.

She asked my husband and me to help her move some stuff out of the house. I couldn't pass up the opportunity. So over we went, one sunny Saturday morning. The house seemed fine, just an old Victorian that, if it were on the east side of the river, would have been fixed up grandly and sold for half a million dollars. Hell, that might be its fate on this side of the river, someday, if its reputation doesn't precede it.

I had thought, when the woman in Kroger was talking, that she made it seem like she had lived in the house many, many years ago. But when we walked through, we saw, just like she'd said, a hope chest in the front bedroom and a closet full of old dresses in the back room.

"What's in here?" my husband asked, knocking on the hope chest.

"I don't know," Helen said. "They didn't give me a key for it. But it needs to go."

"Honey, let's you and me move it by the front door." So he grabbed one end, I grabbed the other, and I swear to you, we could barely lift it. It was so heavy. It took us a good ten minutes to get it out into the front hall.

"How are we going to get that in the truck?" I asked.

My husband just shook his head. "We might have to get some of the guys over here to help me."

The upstairs had been converted to its own apartment, so the grand staircase had been walled off at the top. We went around back and up the outside stairs.

As we were walking into the upstairs apartment,

Helen was telling us about her plans to restore the house back to one home. We heard a noise. It took a minute for me to recognize it, but it was obviously the squealing groan of wood against wood.

We all looked at each other.

And there was the noise again.

My husband and I ran downstairs, ran into the house, and there was the hope chest, not in the hall where we'd left it, but in the bedroom doorway.

"No," my husband said. He stormed down the hallway, checking rooms. "There has got to be someone here."

"There's not," I whispered. I didn't mean to, but I couldn't help it.

"This cannot happen," he said.

Finally, Helen appeared in the doorway. "What was it?"

My husband motioned to the bedroom doorway, almost like he was disgusted.

And then, that damn hope chest moved again. With all of us looking at it, it just slid three inches across the floor.

I screamed and ran outside. They quickly followed.

We all stood there, not sure we should leave, afraid to go back inside.

"What am I going to do?" Helen asked.

"Well, I'd leave that goddamn chest in the bedroom, for starters," my husband said.

April 5th

THE FORT NEGLEY LIGHTS

It's hard to say how long this has been going on and people just didn't know it was a ghost. Until the rise of cell phones, I don't know how you'd know for sure. I first heard about it from some Vandy grad students who lived over on Marlborough, just next to Love Circle, which they regularly walked up to the top of. At night, even in the city, they found it a wonderful spot for star-gazing.

But one evening, at dusk, they were up on top of Love Circle with a friend who was something of a Civil War buff. He was pointing out to them why Love Circle was such a strategic spot, showing them how you could see clear across town, from the Centennial Park dog park hill to the old reservoir that marks where Fort Casino was to Fort Negley.

And as he pointed at Fort Negley, they all saw a faint, blinking light. At first, they thought it was nothing more than maybe a car or, they speculated, kids with flashlights up in the park.

But then the friend said, "I think that's Morse code."

"What's it say?"

"I don't know."

"That's weird."

"Maybe they're doing some kind of reenactment at the fort?"

So they went to see. But the fort was locked and dark.

The couple didn't think anything of it until they saw the light again, this time in the middle of the afternoon.

"Okay, that is something," they said to each other. "Let's go see." They grabbed their binoculars, got in the car and cut over by Rose Park and stopped there to see if they could still see it. And there, in the woods below Fort Negley was a shiny spot of some sort.

"You stay here," Sam said to Lee. "Just keep watching it while I try to get closer." And so Sam took the car over to Fort Negley, staying on the cell phone with Lee the whole way.

"Yes, I can still see it," Lee said. "Go more to your left."

"I can't go any farther left."

"Well, it should be right there."

"Can you see me?"

"Yes, it's right there, right in front of you."

"There's nothing... Oh, excuse me, sir."

And then long silence.

"Honey, are you there?"

Lee searched the hillside through the binoculars and was just about to dial 9-1-1 when Sam ran into the Fort Negley parking lot at full speed.

"What?"

"I thought I saw a man, in a uniform, but he... I don't know... I saw him, but I didn't. His face. It was like he had no face, just nothing where his face should have been."

April 6ᵗʰ

ALL THE SAME OLD HAUNTS

They say that Interstate 40 sliced the heart of the city in two. But the truth is that, as a Southern town, Nashville always had two hearts: Broadway for some folks and Jefferson Street for others. Back before the interstate almost killed it, Jefferson Street between Fisk University and Tennessee State University was home to some of the most amazing music. Folks will still tell you about watching Jimi ("Marbles" at the time) Hendrix drag his amp clear from the Del Morocco to Club Baron to challenge Johnny Jones, and how Johnny Jones handed young Hendrix his ass, back before Marbles became a rock god.

Of course, if everyone who claims to have seen that had actually seen it, half the city would have been empty. Hell, who knows? Maybe a little-known open secret is that half the city used to congregate outside Club Baron just waiting to see what might happen. You'd think, though, if that was the case, someone could have stepped in and helped poor Harold Hebb when he was stabbed, rest his soul.

Most folks will tell you that the Elks Lodge, which is what's there now, is a little unsettling, and I know many of the folks who feel uneasy about it laugh and claim that it must be the ghost of Harold Hebb. And I'm not trying to discount what these folks are saying. I'm just saying that what's going on at the Elks Lodge is stranger than that, because the Elks Lodge is not haunted by a man; it's haunted by the Club Baron.

No, hear me out.

You know that feeling, when you're slightly drunk at a bar with your friends? And you go into the bathroom and do what women do in the bathroom and you come out and you start heading toward the bar and you suddenly realize that you can't find your friends? That moment when you aren't quite sure of where you are or what's going on? And how one of them will call your name, from another part of the room, and wave you over with "We found a table?"

At the Elks Lodge, it is just as common for a woman to come out of the bathroom and find that not only can she not find her friends, but that none of the people before her look familiar to her. Even the room looks different. And quite often she will step back, confused, and believe she has somehow come out of the wrong bathroom door— that maybe there were two exits, one into the room she is supposed to occupy and another into this room. And she'll go back into the bathroom, maybe pat her face and neck with a wet, cool paper towel, and come back out again to find the familiar Elks Lodge. She won't even think to mention to her friends the wrong door and the other room.

But of course, there is no wrong door. It's just that once she came out of the bathroom into Club Baron and the next time she came out into the Elks Lodge.

Other times folks *will* mention it, that for a second they seemed to have gotten lost. And someone at another table will roll his eyes to his friends, and they will all nod, but say nothing.

As far as I can tell, it's very rare for one place to haunt another, so folks have their theories about what is happening. Maybe the Elks Lodge isn't haunted at all. Instead, maybe there's some kind of time anomaly and folks are, just for a few seconds, transported back in time. Two things are brought up to discount this theory, both based on the noticeable differences in how women dress. One, if it is really the 1950s or '60s a person is travelling to, why is no one shocked when this contemporary woman comes out of the bathroom? Wouldn't her outfit be so strange that she would be remarkable? And two, it's not like that was so long ago, and yet no one who frequented the Club Baron back in the day has any recollection of anything strange like that happening. They remember gambling and music and dancing and drinking. But no one remembers oddly dressed women regularly coming out of the bathroom.

Another popular theory is that it's not *exactly* haunted, in that it's not like the souls of the dead are trapped in the Elks Lodge. Instead, the folks in this camp explain, the times folks had in Club Baron were so intense and singular and fun that somehow those moments were imprinted into the building itself and, when the circumstances are right, whatever "right" might be, Club Baron is projected into the Elks Lodge and plays, like a movie plays when you bring light and screen together, with no need for actors to be present. So the Elks Lodge seems haunted, but really you're just seeing what you might call old footage.

I myself don't know. All I do know is that you can't make it happen—a person could walk in and out of the Elks Lodge every day for the rest of his life and never walk into Club Baron—but that it happens frequently enough that only *almost* everyone you meet will think you're crazy if it happens to you.

I know that it happened to a couple of guys who were down here from New York. I won't mention their names, because I know they don't want people to think they're crazy, but one, a black man, is a well-known music producer, and the other is a relatively famous white male musician. At the time, they were still at that stage in their careers where they knew enough about music to be a little foolish. They were, for example, determined while they were down here to find the actual crossroads where Robert Johnson sold his soul to the Devil, because they did not yet know enough to know that there is no crossroads to find because Robert Johnson never did that. And, I suspect, they had no clue how far a drive it is from here to Clarksdale, unless it was worse and they had Clarksdale and Clarksville confused.

Anyway, the two of them were determined to see some of these old clubs and they had asked around at their hotel and no one seemed to be able to help them. They chalked this up to a mixture of Southern stupidity and white people not knowing where the cool places in town were, so they asked for directions to Jefferson Street and, after a long meal with a lot of booze, they set out in that direction. They parked, I believe, in the shopping center there at the corner of 18th and Jefferson and got out and began walking toward TSU.

They must have been a strange sight, even now. Two obviously wealthy men in long, expensive coats, swaying gently as they walked down the street. Stumbling under the interstate, wondering where, in this godforsaken town, they could find a little action. And, finally, there was the Club Baron, lights blazing, music pouring out into the street, people gathered in the doorway.

Maybe if our New York pair had been less drunk, they would have noticed if there were strange stares. But, as it was nothing seemed amiss. They made their way in and were about to sit down when a woman came over and grabbed the producer's elbow.

"Not here," she said. "First, you're early. You know it doesn't start until after one. And second, you know," and here she lowered her voice, "he's going to make folks uncomfortable. Go on upstairs." The two looked at each other, confused but curious. And up the stairs they went.

I think they were expecting a poker game, to hear them tell it, when they do tell it, which is not often. Instead, there were maybe twenty wooden chairs and some tables and, oddly, some instruments—a couple of beat-up guitars against the wall, a trumpet on one of the chairs and a trombone on a stand near a table in the back.

For a few minutes, they just stood there. But nothing happened. So, being musicians at heart, they both slipped out of their heavy coats, threw them over a chair, picked up the guitars, tested them out, made some tuning adjustments, and began to pick out some melodies.

After a while, other men carrying cases started arriving, up the staircase our duo had come up, and from a staircase that seemed to lead directly out back. At first all the men were black, but after instruments had been unpacked and small talk finished and beer and cigarettes passed around, white men began arriving, too. And only a few people seemed to know each other, but they all seemed friendly.

"I saw you at the Subway Lounge," a white man said, shaking hands with a black man, "What were you doing with your hand on that solo? Can you show me?"

Or, "When I was in London, there was a man who, when he played the trumpet, would mute it with his beer bottle, like this…" and everyone would turn to watch and then the folks who could play trumpet would give it a try.

Or they would all play songs they knew, together. And though our pair didn't know those songs, they would strum along, thrilled to be watching talented men play together. And that was the whole night. There was some sense that it was crucial that they break things up before daylight, that they didn't want to be caught together. But the Producer and the Musician at the time just took this to mean that there might be trouble with wives or girlfriends if they were out clear into the next day.

And so, after a few hours, our duo said their goodbyes to their new friends, insisted that folks look them up in New York if they every found themselves that way and made their way into the street. Now, the Producer will tell you, if he tells you the story at all, that looking back, it should have been that moment that tipped them off, because when they got out on the street, it was dead silent. And they should have heard the leaving noises of the men who should have been coming out of the club with them. But they were so caught up in recounting for each other the best parts of the night that they didn't notice they were alone.

And, of course, when they tried to come back the

next night, they found only the Elks Lodge, and not the club they had been in the night before.

April 7th

THE BRENTWOOD LIBRARY

I don't think there's anyone in town who doesn't remember this. It started bad enough. When they went to break ground for the Brentwood library, right across the road from the giant, narrow steel diamond of the WSM radio tower, they found Native American remains. And so construction was delayed while the city and the activists argued over what to do. It ended up costing the developers a bunch of money, but eventually the remains were relocated and construction continued.

And then, when they were digging the foundation for the back part of the building, rumor has it that they found more bones. But this time the general contractor told the workers to shut up about it and keep building. No more delays. Not for dead folks who couldn't bother to show up when the dead-folk moving was being done. And so, people say, the Brentwood library went up on top of Native American graves.

It was little surprise, then, when the voices started. Faint voices you'd hear on site. You might have a long two-by-four slung over your shoulder, walking down a steel beam and, there, in broad daylight, two stories up, you would hear a woman's voice, faint but clear. Or sometimes a man's deep voice, softly singing.

The men who were part of the crew from the beginning quit, sure that the voices were the dead people. Even a crew they brought in from Kentucky lasted only three days.

And this was not your typical haunting. Everyone on site eventually heard it. Someone brought a pastor in to pray over the site. No luck. Someone else suggested they call in the activists to have them work their magic and appease the spirits. But no one wanted to risk being required to tear down the library. And so the work continued.

Then one day, an electrician turned to a plumber and asked, "That voice? Isn't that Ricky Skaggs? Ricky Skaggs ain't dead, is he?"

And the plumber stopped, cocked his head and, after a second, said, "That sure does sound like Ricky Skaggs."

And the electrician looked at the plumber and began to laugh. "This whole place is just one big radio, ain't it? We're listening to WSM."

The plumber laughed in return. "I think you're right."

And that seems to be the case. When the atmospheric conditions are right, the metal in the Brentwood library acts like a giant radio receiver. So, when you're alone in the stacks and you hear faint music, it's just those same old Nashville ghosts, the folks who always haunt us.

DEAD AND GONE

In the old City Cemetery, if you turn right down the first lane once you get in, you'll see a large monument with no writing on it. The sides of the stone, where the words should go, have been worn clean. Or so it appears.

The first person who told me the story of this monument told me that it went like this: a young couple— very well-to-do, very much in love—had gotten married, as folks did. And quickly discovered that the woman was pregnant. They couldn't have been happier.

Sadly, their happiness was short-lived. The woman died in childbirth. But, before she did, she made the husband promise he would never remarry.

That tomb is hers, and on its side the husband had carved the most heartbreaking ode to his love for his wife.

But it's not easy for a man to raise a little girl by himself, and eventually he did remarry, not out of love, but out of wanting to provide a mother for his daughter.

It is said that on the day of his wedding, the stone crumbled and his words of love fell off.

Or the story goes like this: he was a terrible husband, who beat his wife regularly, and she could find no refuge from him. Folks knew, as they do, but they didn't think it was their business.

And then he killed her.

He didn't mean to, of course, or so he told himself. She could have kept her mouth shut. She could have had his dinner ready on time. She could have had it ready later. He couldn't remember why he was mad, just that he had hit her and hit her and hit her until she stopped moving. And he had thought, when she finally stopped, struggling, "Yes, that's right. You just take it."

But she wasn't just taking it. She was dead.

He wasn't sure what would happen next. He was wealthy, but so was her father. He might be hanged. In desperation, he carried her body up to the top of the grand staircase, and threw it down. Then he stripped off his clothes and threw them in the fire. He could hear the slave girl calling from the back yard. She would find his wife, find him. She would know.

He began to yell, "Go for help! Go for help! She's jumped."

The slave girl didn't know, of course. She had been in the garden and had seen nothing. But she knew enough about him to be shocked, but unsurprised, to hear that the wife had committed suicide.

The husband played the grieving widower to the hilt, put up a lavish monument in the city cemetery with grand words of love written all over it.

And then, almost as soon as the last word was carved, the first word began to fade. The worker who noticed it said it was like a slow, wet rag on a chalkboard.

The husband paid, for a while, to have the stone recarved. Every time the words came off. But eventually everyone in town came to believe the wife wouldn't stand to have him lie on her grave. So it remains bare to this day.

And lately, I have heard it told like this. That two young women were in love, though the times being what they were they did not know to call it that. They would spend their afternoons wrapped in each other's limbs and everyone in town jokingly called them the two wives.

You have to understand how it was back then. No one, least of all the two wives, took their love very seriously. They would go on to marry men. Love often didn't enter into it. And it never occurred to them to even consider spending their lives together. It just wouldn't have.

Both were married off to suitable men, men they both found to be fine, though they still saw each other when they could and wrote each other when they couldn't. Then one of them became pregnant and, sadly, it killed her.

The other was distraught.

The husband buried the dead wife in an elaborate tomb in the city cemetery and had great words of love carved on it.

And, when she could, the other wife would visit the grave. Often she was so overcome with grief that she would trace over the words the husband had had carved. And often she was furious that the husband's words would stand as the truth, and her love would go unacknowledged.

So she slowly began to chip them away, those words that should have been hers. And just as slowly, it's said, a ghostly figure helped her. Now, they say, when you drive by the cemetery, you will often see two young women in long, full skirts, walking arm-in-arm among the stones, admiring the flowers, stealing a kiss.

The truth is that there never was any writing on the tomb. The uneven surface is not from words falling away, but from a century or so of rain and pollution wearing at the sandstone. Once you know this, it's impossible to look at the marker and see anything but that truth.

And yet people would rather believe anything but that, rather hear any story of heartbreak and haunts.

Make of that what you will.

April 9th

PRESSED INTO SERVICE

Jesse Price was an ordinary guy who died when he was twenty-six in a train accident in 1880 on Valentine's Day. If there was speculation about his death being more suicide than accident, based on the day, let me put that to rest now: Price just died, in the way people just die.

He lay in the ground unbothered for quite some time. What he thought about, if anything, we don't know.

This, though, we do know: we know of a girl, a young girl, so desperate for good fortune, for her boyfriend to return from the war in one piece, that in the middle of the night, she parked her car back behind the far wall, walked nervously up Oak Street (and for good reason; that part of town was, back then, not that safe even during the day) and, when she felt sure there were no cars about to come by, slinked over the fence.

She was looking for her family plot, to beg a dead great aunt for help.

But imagine, you're in an ancient cemetery at night, stumbling around with only a small flashlight you need to keep pointed down if you don't want to attract the attention of neighbors or the police. Every twig snap, every shadow shift, and soon she was terrified out of her mind. And there, before her, was Mr. Price's grave.

"Oh, please," she whispered, "For Christ's sake, bring Donny home." And then, she found a small stone nearby and made a small mark, a cross on the back of his grave.

And this tells you a lot about the kind of person Mr. Price was, because Donny came home.

I was there with a medium on the annual October tour, and when we walked by Mr. Price's grave, she laughed.

"Oh my," she said to no one in particular, "That hasn't worked out."

"What's that?" I asked.

"Mr. Price feels very fondly toward these folks who have worked so hard to clean the place up. He has, whenever someone has marked his grave, done the one thing he can think to keep them from marking it again."

"Oh?"

"He's tried to make what they've asked for happen, so that they won't come back."

"Ah, I see what you mean. Has he considered stopping?"

"Not lately. By now, he kind of likes feeling useful again."

April 10th

I admit, when the woman from the Downtown Presbyterian church said, "We never have crying babies on Sunday morning," it was out of my mouth before I could stop it, "Do y'all have *any* babies in church on Sunday morning?"

Luckily, she thought that was funny.

To look at it, you would assume that the Downtown Presbyterian Church, if haunted at all, is haunted by the Civil War soldiers who died in it when it was used as a hospital.

But no, instead it is haunted by an old man they affectionately call "Granddad," who has a kind of shambling way of walking, who is often seen sitting in the pew on Sunday morning or coming down the center aisle after the service, leaning over the ends of pews as if picking up the bulletins and attendance pads left behind.

Some folks thought he wasn't really a ghost, just a memory the building has of an old usher.

But one morning a young mother was sitting in her pew, her baby in the carrier beside her. The baby, as babies often do, began to fuss. The mother turned to her left to dig through her bag to get a pacifier when she heard the faint but unmistakable sound of keys jingling.

And then the baby laughed.

Of course, she assumed it was one of the other congregants, entertaining the baby, but when she turned to thank whoever it was, the pew was empty.

April 11ᵗʰ

THE BROKEN MIRROR

Depending on when you visit the Hooters in Hermitage, sometimes there's a mirror behind the bar. This is not the strange part. If you ask about it when it's not there, they'll tell you that the mirror broke and they're debating about whether to get a new one.

What's strange is what exactly they mean by "broke."

See, because no matter what mirror they put up there, eventually there comes to be one too many waitresses in it. Say it's in the middle of the afternoon and you have two girls covering, one with brown hair and one with red. If you're just looking around the restaurant, you'll see them running around, lifting trays over patrons' heads, leaning over to pour more iced tea, checking narrow black folders to make sure they've got the right ticket for the table before setting it down.

But, if you look in the mirror, as often as not, you'll also see a small blonde with a high ponytail and an enormous friendly smile, darting from table to table.

The staff is usually split 50/50 about how they feel about her. Some of them are terrified, even though she only appears in the mirror and there aren't weird noises or a feeling like anyone else is present if you're alone in the dining room. There's nothing at all creepy about her.

Some of them secretly appreciate, on busy days, when they are so tired of the "clever" comments and the small tips, catching her eye in the mirror and getting a supportive nod or wink.

But eventually the patrons notice. And then it becomes really weird. Usually, one person will see her first, and he'll say something just to the folks at his table. You'll see them looking at the mirror and then kind of sitting tall in their seats to crane their necks around and check if they aren't perhaps mistaken.

Their weird behavior will get the attention of other people, who will see what they see in the mirror, and soon enough, the whole restaurant grinds to a silent halt. No one eats. No one speaks. They all are just watching the small blonde in the mirror.

They say that one time she seemed to notice that they had all stopped to stare at her and she looked out at them, her brow furrowed in confusion, and she smiled and shrugged, like "What are y'all looking at?" and went back about her business.

On that day, everyone ran out of the restaurant in terror.

This was, you can imagine, a nightmare. Tabs remained open. Credit cards were left unclaimed. Meals were never paid for. The mirror was taken down, brought out into the parking lot, and busted into countless sparkling pieces.

They've tried new mirrors, but she's always in them, working away like it's the most ordinary thing in the world.

*April 12*th

THE HOME DEPOT PARKING LOT

Weirdly enough, the ghosts in the Inglewood Home Depot parking lot may be the most upsetting ghosts in town. They don't do anything particularly scary. They tend to walk across the open grassy area between the parking lot and the road, looking around like something is missing, and then they stand in the parking lot, looking confused or shaking their heads or standing with one hand on their hips and the other wiping the sweat off their brows.

Sometimes they will turn to each other and converse, pointing to the empty space and gesturing about the general size and shape of the missing landmark.

The singer is still recognizable to people, and so his presence is the most upsetting. When they tore down the house, people said softly to each other, so no one else could hear, "Well, at least Mr. Reeves isn't alive to see this."

And yet, there he is, with Rev. Craighead and the Bradfords, standing in the parking lot, looking, for all intents and purposes, like folks who wish, just one more time, they could see a ghost.

April 13*th*

THE STRANGE CASE OF SCENIC DRIVE

There's nothing unusual about the house on Scenic Drive. Scenic Drive itself is quiet. On one side of the street is a wooded lot where people often walk their dogs. On the other side are long, oversized brick ranches. And this one is no different. It sits at the top of a hill and has, by all accounts, a cheerful disposition.

Still, most dogs still won't go in the front yard. There's a way that the hillside is cut away that suggests something hidden, and you'd think that the dogs would be curious, but they're not. Most will, if given the opportunity, cross the street to avoid going too close.

It is, strangely enough, the old bear cave. When the zoo was out here, this is where the bears were.

And the story goes that they will still follow you, those bears.

It's a rite of passage for Lipscomb students to walk alone in the dark down that street, starting at Glendale Lane and heading north. If you are brave enough, your friends will wait for you where Scenic hooks to the right and becomes Tower Place and cheer you on.

Most kids never get that far. They say they hear the noises coming from the cave and they either turn back toward Glendale or, if they are too far, they'll scramble through the wooded lot back toward campus.

This has lead to a companion ghost story, of a lone young college student, who, if female, had just gotten engaged and was walking to her parents' home to tell them the news when she was hit by a car. So violent was the impact that the ring went flying and was never recovered. Or if male, that he was walking to his beloved's parents' home to ask them for her hand in marriage when he was hit by a car. And so on.

In either case, it is said that if you drive down Scenic at night, often you see him or her walking slowly down the street, searching for that ring.

April 14th

It works best if you have two young, suggestible preteen girls in your back seat. You take them to Bobbie's Dairy Dip and then start filling their heads with ghost stories about Adelicia Acklen. It doesn't matter which stories you choose to tell.

Start with the ones about how greedy she was and so she never left her home because she couldn't bear to be without her things. Go on to the ones about how she sold her soul to the Devil in exchange for prosperity, even in the darkest days of war and reconstruction, and so is doomed to walk the land.

Or tell them about her grief for her dead children and how she cannot bear to leave them behind.

Just tell those stories as you drive across town toward Mount Olivet Cemetery. As you're pulling up the long drive, be sure to tell them how people have seen her figure around her mausoleum. And yes, you're going to have to explain what a mausoleum is.

But it will be worth it when you pull up in front of the Acklen mausoleum and you dare them to go take a peek in and you make like you're going with them, but you hang back.

They walk toward the door. The closer they get, the slower they go. Slower and slower until finally they are pushing each other and daring each other to look in.

And they do.

And they will see the figure and they will scream.

And you're laughing, because you know it's just a statue—a marble angel.

But when you hear the laughter of another woman,

and you look around and see there's no one there but you, then, maybe you're the one who's screaming next.

JINN MONEY

I had met with little success finding anyone in Antioch who would tell me a ghost story. Finally, a friend of a friend said he knew a Kurdish woman who had lived in Antioch when she first immigrated and who could tell me a story from her time there that would freak me out.

I met her in a little restaurant in a strip mall tucked behind a car dealership. Her daughter-in-law came with her, but, other than exchanging brief pleasantries with me, she said nothing once her mother-in-law began to speak.

This is the story my informant told me:

"When we first came here, they told us to keep to ourselves—that people here didn't care to understand that we weren't terrorists. But the apartment we lived in, the walls were so thin that we could hear our neighbor crying when her husband was gone.

"My husband and I decided that I should talk to her, if I had the chance. And so I waited. And then one day, I came out onto my balcony to water the plants and I saw her on her balcony, just standing there, looking out over the parking lot.

"'How are you doing?' I asked. I startled her.

"'Not so good,' she said.

"She told me how they had come to Nashville from the east, how back home her husband was the best guitar player around. But here? How did she put it? 'Back home he was one in a million. Here he's one out of a million.'

"That's how I knew," the black-eyed woman said to me.

"Knew?" I asked.

51

"That was a very clever thing, don't you agree?"

"Well, yeah," I had laughed even just hearing it.

"Here you will often see women married to men who are... I'm sorry, but there is no good way to say this."

"Hey, you're not going to offend me. Go ahead."

"I see women like my old neighbor—very clever, very sweet, very talented. A good husband would find a way for his wife to use those talents. But here he was, taking all of her good things.

"He didn't know that she was better than him. But she worked two jobs so that he could make his music. And she turned the money over to him so that he could pay the bills.

"One evening, I saw her standing by her car, crying, an envelope in her hand.

"'What's wrong?' I asked her. And she told me how she had been at the store, trying to buy bread and milk, and her check card would not work. And here was a notice from the people who ran the apartment complex saying they were behind on their rent.

"I brought her inside and I put her at my kitchen table. I said, 'Here is some bread. Here is some money for milk. You keep it. You keep the money.'

"'No,' she said, 'I can't take your money.' But I sat down across from her and I said, 'My grandmother told me a story when I was a little girl. In it was a woman who, every time she laughed, had jewels fall from her mouth. Giggles would produce jewels fit for rings; belly laughs would cause her to burp up a great gem, the size of an egg. And a jinn came to know of her gift and he kidnapped her. "You will laugh for me," he said, "so that I can be rich." But she found nothing about her situation funny. She was so terrified that she couldn't laugh, only cry. And so he cast a spell on her. He said it was to help her laugh; to help her do what God had

52

intended for her.

"'And so, when he put a stick in her side, she would laugh and dance and jewels would spill out of her mouth. When he removed the stick, she would fall into a deep sleep. It was a terrible life for her, though she laughed every day.'

"I waited to see if my neighbor understood.

"She said to me, 'Something's wrong with his teeth.'

"I didn't know what this meant, but when I told my husband about it, he nodded and said, 'I noticed her husband's smell.'

"When I saw my neighbor again, she said that she had called her mother for money, but her mother refused to send any; said that she had talked to her pastor about her daughter's situation and the pastor had said that a woman must leave her family and cleave to her husband. Whatever they were going through was God's will.

"I gave her another ten dollars, slipped it into her purse when she wasn't looking.

"When I saw her again, she looked terrible. Her face was so pale and she could barely meet my eyes.

"'What happened?' I asked.

"'I prayed,' she said, 'I prayed so hard for help. And there's no answer. No one is coming to help me. Not my parents. Not even God. I just wish my granny were here, you know?'

"So when I saw the old woman, I thought nothing of it. She was sitting out on the balcony while the couple was away.

"'Hello,' I said.

"'What kind of place is this?' the old woman asked. 'Each apartment is like a box. Each building is like a box made up of boxes. Each box sits next to other boxes, all over the hill, as far as you can see. I ain't never seen so many places for people to live, and so few people.'

"'I believe they are at work,' I said.

"And then, finally, she said, 'I know you are the only one who's been nice to my baby since she came here. I know you put money in her purse. I know you feed her. I know you watch out for her. And I will make it square with you. I just have one favor to ask you. If you hear a knock on your door, open it.'

"'Of course,' I said.

"It was many weeks later when there was a knock on our door. It was very late at night, and so my husband went to open it. And there in the hall was the husband, with three other men, and the husband was fumbling to get his key in his door. My husband and I came out into the hall and we made such a fuss over him, helped him get the door open, and when we got inside, I ran to the bedroom and woke my neighbor up.

"'Your grandmother sent me to help you,' I said. 'Now get up and come stay the night with us.'

"'But my granny is dead,' she said. Now I was very shocked by this, because I had talked to her, but I still insisted.

"'Come stay with us.' And she did. We never found out for certain what happened in the apartment that night, but the husband was murdered. Our dear neighbor certainly would have been, too, if she had remained there. And think of that knock. Who was knocking on our door?"

"Wow," I said, "That gave me chills."

"That is not the strangest part," she said. "Many months after the neighbor moved away, I found a jar of these dimes on my kitchen table." She pulled an old dime out of her pocket and handed it over to me. "At least fifty dollars in dimes. At the time those dimes were in circulation, fifty dollars must have been a lot of money for a family."

"That's a Mercury dime," I said.

"So?"

"Do they all look like this?" I said.

"Yes. Why?"

"That jar's worth a lot of money to your family now."
I laughed. "Wow, a ghost left money for your family."

"Oh, no," she said. "There's no such thing as ghosts."

Years later, long after my informant was dead, I ran
into her daughter-in-law at the post office. She told me that
her daughter had recently come home from a high school
party drunk. She and her husband were furious and the
daughter said, "But Grandmother drank! You think I don't
know?"

They looked at each other, very confused.

"What are you talking about?" my informant's son
asked.

"Those dimes we aren't allowed to touch?
Grandmother's gin money?"

"No, no, sweetie," the daughter-in-law said, "That's
money a jinn gave your grandmother. That's why we keep it
locked away."

April 16th

LET ME CALL YOU SWEETHEART

"Lookaway" is the name of the old house on Manila Street. It was a wedding gift from Mr. Whitson to his new bride, Beth Slater Whitson. You have probably never heard of her. When the house was for sale a couple of years ago, the listing made no mention of her ever having lived there. The last thing anyone who wants to sell that house wants to do is to draw attention to Mrs. Whitson.

Of course, after a while, you can't help but notice her. You'll come home to find your clean pots out of the cupboard and arranged on the kitchen stove. You'll be sitting in the living room reading a book, and the television will come on and start to flip through channels. Lights will be on in rooms you know you left dark.

And sometimes the air will hang heavy with the smell of magnolia blossoms, even with the windows shut, even when the magnolias aren't in bloom.

Even the neighborhood children who use the huge front yard like a neighborhood park will come home singing "Let me call you sweetheart, I'm in love with you. Let me hear you whisper that you love me, too." And when their mothers ask, "Did you make that up?" the children say, "No, that woman in the funny dress sings it when she's on the porch."

And, by this point, the mothers don't even bother to look out their windows in suspicion.

"It's like this," one says to me. "I don't want to live there and I would scream if I ever saw her, but she's kind of our neighbor, so what can you do? I heard they called in a pastor to bless the place, but he said he didn't think she was evil or trapped there. She's just where she wants to be. There's nothing he can do. Just wait for her to move on."

"Or be forgotten?"

"How are you going to forget someone who's teaching your kids those old-fashioned songs? Did you listen to what I told you?"

April 17th

THE WAIT

In a little house on Venus Drive, she waited for him to come home from the war. She passed the time making airplanes, and when he got home he told all his friends that she was a better mechanic than anyone in town. His car ran because of her expertise.

Telling you that much, if you're old enough, you can probably guess who they were.

They had the kind of love everyone hopes for. Two young people devoted to each other, growing older together.

He said to her, often, "I will never leave you. Never."

And she would say, "You can't promise that. What if you die?"

"Even if I die, if there's a way, I will be here."

"Me, too, mister," she would say, "me, too."

She died. Got hit by a car while she was out riding her bike. He was at home, sensed nothing amiss. Even when the police finally came to his door, he smiled much longer than was appropriate, because he simply could not believe she would leave him.

He waited all evening for her to come back in the door, to tell him it was all a mistake.

She never came.

Every holiday, he waited for some sign.

"Dad," their daughter would say, "open the present."

"Oh, I'm sorry. I thought I heard something," he would lie. He never heard anything.

When his grandson was born, he thought, "This is it, if she comes, it will be now." And he waited for anything he

59

could consider to be her: a noise, an out of place shadow, the smell of her perfume. But nothing.

He met a woman at church, and eventually it seemed to make sense that they would get married. Still, he didn't want to offend his dead wife. "If you mind," he would whisper, "just tell me."

But nothing.

His son-in-law was kind of a jerk. He would say things like, "Maybe she's too busy. Maybe she's got better things to do. Maybe she's forgotten all about you."

But he felt sure if she could come back, she would have.

She never did.

Finally, after years, with his second wife by his side, he died.

It went like this. He had been semi-conscious for hours, not quite able to do much more than mumble. And then he sat up, looked ahead of him, and said plain as day, "Oh, so that's why," and started to sob.

And then, after a minute he lay back down and fell asleep. He never regained consciousness.

April 18ᵗʰ

THE HENDERSONVILLE TREE

I think it's apparent to anyone who has had a cat that cats saunter easily between here and the hereafter and back again. Many live cats disappear outdoors and appear days later in a closet that hasn't been opened in weeks, their ability to walk through walls already well mastered before they shake loose of their skin.

Once they have passed on, again, it is nothing for them to slip back here and be seen, regularly, even by people who never knew them in life, napping in a favorite sunbeam or sitting in the window.

Even the most rational people have been known to settle into bed and feel the weight of a cat on the blankets near their feet, even if they have never owned a cat.

Dogs, on the other hand, though well-known for noticing the dead, tend not to spend too much time while living bothering with them. Dead dogs, being easily distracted, tend only to haunt the kitchen, if they bother with haunting anywhere. Many people report hearing the clinking of nails on linoleum or the soft, silvery click of a license on a collar in the kitchen long after a dog has passed on.

Dogs don't really feel regret, other than about not getting that one piece of steak they really wanted, and so they aren't often ghosts. They die and things catch their attention and they are off after a new scent or a movement in the bush. By the time they think to circle back home, there you are, dead yourself.

Sometimes a dog will haunt *with* you. They are loyal that way.

But I can't help but wonder about other things. Does every living thing have the ability to haunt, once it's dead? Is there such a thing as a ghost chicken?

I admit, I laugh at the thought of a ghost chicken. But then you hear stories about how a momma chicken will throw her whole body over a brood of chicks to protect them from owls, even if it might mean her own death. And you wonder—is there something about even a chicken that might linger?

But what about a ghost jellyfish? Or a phantom amoeba? A haunting mushroom?

Some things are impossible to imagine.

I would have never thought of a ghostly tree, even though there's something very person-y, though utterly inhuman, about the trees in my yard, always looking like mad scientist, about to convene out by the creek.

But I've heard of just such a case up in Hendersonville, in a subdivision just off New Shackle Island Road, which I will leave unnamed so that they are not inundated with looky-loos.

Before the subdivision was built, there was an ancient oak standing in a field. Four people joining hands could barely stretch around it. It was in terrible shape. Parts were dead and parts were dying. Twice, during one spring, huge branches broke off and crashed to the ground with such force people nearby called the police, thinking the noise was some kind of explosion.

Still, it was something to see; ancient and wild, thick with leaves that often seemed to move as much with the memory of old breezes as with anything you could feel under it.

Sadly, though understandably, once it was obvious that the field was destined for houses, the tree was chopped down.

That does not stop the tree from casting shadows on the houses near where it once stood. I have been in a back bedroom, looked out a south-facing window onto a sunny back yard, and I have seen that there is no sunlight in that bedroom, as if something still blocks the light. I have heard there's a kitchen in which you could even make out the dappled shapes of the shadows of leaves on the floor in front of the patio door. The builder, free of charge, put a tree right in front of the patio doors, so it is now not so apparent that those shadows have nothing to make them.

And I can't explain it. They say there are two types of ghosts. Some are actual sentient beings, who either can't or won't move on. Others, they say, are like memories, held in a place by means we don't yet understand, which play out like old movies when the conditions are right.

Who knows which the Hendersonville tree is? Either it remembers that it was once alive or that place remembers it. It's hard to know how much of a difference there is between either scenario.

April 19th
THE GHOST WHO THOUGHT YOU WERE LYING

Kenny Robertson's dad had a tough death. Toward the end, Kenny moved him into Kenny's house and set up the hospital bed in the living room. Kenny arranged him so he could see the TV if he turned one way and out the picture window if he turned the other way.

Their fights went something like this:

"Bring me a beer."

"You can't be drinking beer with your pills, Dad."

"What? I might die? I'm fucking dying, Kenny. Bring me a goddamn beer."

"No, Dad."

"Bring me a goddamn beer. Fuck it."

"We're out of beer."

"Bullshit."

Or:

"Can't I have something better than this shit to eat? What about some chips?"

"The doctor says you can't have all that salt."

"Kenny, I'm fucking dying. Chips don't make no goddamn difference."

"It makes a difference to me. I have to wipe your ass."

"You think that's easy for me? Letting your own son wipe your ass? You just wait until it's your turn."

"I'd shoot myself."

"It's easy to think so," his dad said, finally sighing deeply and turning toward the window.

The fights were not easy on either of them, but Kenny preferred them to the long periods of silence when his dad would just stare off into space, like he was practicing being dead.

When he finally did die, he was asleep. He let out a loud, surprised yell that woke Kenny up, but by the time Kenny got into the living room and got the light on, his dad was breathing out for the last time.

"There's nothing that can prepare you for it," Kenny said. "I mean, you say 'he's gone,' but man, until you see it, how it's like he's there one second and then... I don't know. It was like I couldn't recognize him. Like his whole face changed. They said it'd be like he went to sleep. But when you sleep, you still look like yourself. I don't know. It sucked."

After the funeral, Kenny came home, opened the fridge, took out a beer and settled onto the couch. He hadn't had more than four swigs from the beer before he was asleep.

"You know how it is," he said. "It's like, you're just doing this and going this place and that place. I mean, it was like the first time since he died that I really got to stop and just be still. I crashed."

He has a strange look on his face as he starts to tell this next part, as if you can be amused and afraid at the same time.

"When I woke up, every fucking cabinet in the kitchen was wide open. The refrigerator was wide open. And that case of beer was set right in the middle of the floor.

"Yeah, I guess I could have been so tired I sleep-walked. But I woke up with my beer still in my hand. I somehow sleepwalked and didn't spill a drop?

"I think it was him. I think that son of a bitch was like 'No beer? I see plenty of beer now that I'm not stuck in that bed.' Shoot, he was probably searching for chips.

"Nothing like that's happened since. I think that was just his way of saying goodbye, and, you know, letting me know he knew I was a liar."

April 20th

FISK MEMORIAL CHAPEL

One of the nicest spirits in Nashville lingers at Fisk Memorial Chapel. Most of the time, she is more noticed in her absence than her presence. You'll walk into the empty chapel and the air will still be humming, as if someone has just finished playing the organ. Or you will shuffle into your spot in the choir loft and there will be the faint smell of rose water, as if a woman was standing there just seconds before you.

The reason she is one of Nashville's most beloved ghosts has everything to do with the women's restroom. You see, to get into the women's restroom, you open a door on the north side of the vestibule, and immediately you must step down a set of stairs. These stairs are incredibly steep, each step so shallow you think your whole foot might not fit on it, and then the whole thing takes a sharp turn to the left at the bottom, into the actual restroom itself.

No matter how sure-footed you are, if you are in heels, taking those stairs is taking your life into your own hands. And yet, if you are at the chapel for any length of time, you will have to take those stairs.

And, often, as you have your right hand stretched down the wall to steady yourself and your left hand is out behind you, tightly wrapped around the banister, and you are half-leaning forward to see if anyone will need to squeeze by you on the way up, just at the moment you feel like you are about to tip forward and end up sprawled in a broken heap at the bottom of the stairs, you will feel a firm but gentle grip on your arm, a kind fellow visitor setting you right again.

But, of course, when you turn to look, to thank your rescuer, the steep stairway is empty.

Some people have been known to leave gifts of

appreciation for her on those steps, but I must implore you not to make them any more dangerous to traverse than they already are.

April 21ˢᵗ
THE MAN IN THE HOUSE ON SIGLER STREET

It was well-known that Dalt Patton's wife haunted their house. They had fallen in love young. She was nineteen, he twenty-four when they got married. Their first child was stillborn just a month after Mrs. Patton's 20th birthday. And then, for whatever reason, it seemed like they could not have children.

Everyone agreed that this was a terrible tragedy in itself. They were such a beautiful couple.

Sometimes, when he would get home from work, she would be down at the park, talking with the mothers in the neighborhood, watching their children play, and she would seem to almost sense that he was on his way and she would take off running for the house.

Everyone got such a kick out of that, watching a woman in full skirts, hiking her petticoats out of the way and running full bore for home. "Oh, young married folks," they would say. "Do you remember when we were like that?" And they would all laugh and smile.

Her death was so terrible. He came home from work and found her in a broken heap at the bottom of the grand staircase. The one shoe still on her foot was broken at the heel. And it turned out she was pregnant.

He was only thirty-eight, but he never remarried.

"She was my gal," he would say, sitting in the porch swing, a glass of whiskey sweating in his hand. "She was my best gal."

Patton couldn't even bear to throw out her clothes.

"I like feeling like she's still here," he said, though to most folks it was apparent she still was. People would see lights on in the house when he wasn't there. When he was there and people were visiting, they would swear they could hear her laughter in the kitchen.

"Dalt," they would ask. "Is that your wife?" and he would tear up and nod. For the whole rest of his long life he lived there, with little changed since she passed. He stayed there with the ghost of the one woman he ever loved; with the woman he dearly, dearly missed.

April 22ⁿᵈ

THE CHURCH STREET MAN

There have probably always been a lot of ghosts downtown, since it's the oldest part of town, but until folks started moving back down there in great numbers, you only ever heard about the ghosts haunting the honky-tonks.

The gentleman in tonight's story might always have been running down Church Street, a look of exhilaration and terror on his face. The bride, in her great white dress may always have been waiting on the steps of First Presbyterian, every late night, for decades.

But until the moment when Berta Morris decided she didn't really want tbe cab driver to know where she lived, until she decided, at two in the morning, to get out of the cab at Sixth and Church and just walk herself the rest of the way, no one, as far as I know, had seen the couple.

She said at first it seemed normal enough. It was foggy, yes, but the whole spring had been so wet, and patches of fog had ways of just swirling up out of manholes or rolling down the street, like just one more city fixture. It was so ubiquitous it had long since stopped being spooky.

And she didn't even think anything of it as she heard the footsteps behind her; someone obviously running up the street.

It wasn't until she saw the woman on the steps of First Presbyterian that she started to get chills. It was if the woman stepped into existence right in front of her, just one foot into the real world, followed by the other, like a person stepping through a set of curtains at the break.

And then, Berta heard the man shouting, "Jenny, Jenny, wait! Don't do this."

And Jenny smiled as she turned toward the sound of the footsteps.

"I could hear him the whole time," Berta said. "But it was only as he got almost to her that I could see him. And the first thing she said to him was 'You came back.' I thought, at first, I was watching the past. Like something had happened a long time ago and I was just looking through some kind of window onto it.

"But then he turned and looked at me, a huge goofy grin on his face, and he said, 'Ma'am...' Okay, listen, I'm not sure what he said. I thought he said, 'Ma'am, this was the best day of my life.'"

April 23rd

SHADOW LANE

Lainey had a house on Shadow Lane. Like all the houses on Shadow Lane, it was the ubiquitous 1950s brick ranch with two bedrooms, a bathroom and a surprisingly cheery disposition.

In spite of all the house had going for it, it had one thing working against it—it was haunted. Noticeably.

You could be sitting in the living room and watch the light in the dining room come on, followed by the light in the kitchen. Then the kitchen light goes out. And then the dining room light. As if someone has gone in to get a drink and come back.

You could be sitting reading a book, and the television would come on, flip through the channel, and turn itself off.

And things you wouldn't think twice about took on more ominous meanings. You might find a glass of water on a table, waiting for you, and though you wanted a glass of water, you didn't remember getting it.

Sure, maybe you did it without really thinking about it, just a matter of routine.

But if you're alone in the house, of course, there is no one to tell you if you brought the glass in there or if it just appeared.

It got so that Lainey was afraid to be in the house at all.

But her neighbor insisted she call an electrician.

"Are your outlets two-pronged or three?" The neighbor asked.

"Two," she said.

"That's right. You probably got original wiring in

there. Get an electrician."

So she searched the internet, as folks do, for nearby electricians, and the first one to catch her eye was Adams & Sons. And so she called, and the appointment was made for a week from Wednesday.

On that Wednesday, there was a knock at the door and a lanky man in his mid-fifties introduced himself as John Adams.

"My dad was a real history buff," he said. "We wired these houses when they first went in, would you believe it? I have a pretty good sense of all the ways they go wrong."

He immediately got to work, poking around in the fuse box and crawling around in the attic.

About an hour later, Adams found Lainey in her home office.

"Well, ma'am," he said, "I found the immediate problem. At one point, it looks like you had some mice in the attic and they were chewing on some wires up there. Stripped them bare in spots. I believe when those bare wires touched, for whatever reason, they were flickering the lights.

"You're going to need to rewire the house. But I've got that patched up to hold you. Shoot, you're lucky there wasn't a fire. I found some singed insulation already."

"Oh no!" Lainey said.

"You call back over to my boys," Adams said. "Tell them you're going to need the whole house done. They'll work you a deal."

"Great. How much do I owe you?"

"Nothing," he said. "It was treat enough to get back into one of these places and see how it held up. Pretty good, I think, if this is the first trouble you're having. And rewiring the house will cost you more than enough. Don't worry about it."

So, Lainey called Adams & Sons once again and identified herself and gave her address.

"I'm calling because I need you guys to come over."

"Yes, ma'am. We expect to have someone there today."

"Oh, yeah, he's been here already."

"He has?"

"Yes. He came by and fixed some mouse damage and said to call you and tell you we need the whole house rewired."

"Ma'am? Are you sure?"

"Well, yes, he just left. Why?"

"Well, because Adams & Sons is really just me and my brother since my dad died in 2003. I say 'we' like I'm just the guy in the office. But Bob's on vacation, so Adams & Sons today is just me. And I haven't been to your house yet."

"Oh my God. Should I call the police? I let this strange man into my house. I should have known 'John Adams' was made up."

"He said his name was John Adams?"

"Yes."

"That's my dad's name."

And when he got to the house, he did indeed find that the repair had been made. So who knows? Most times either one of them tells you this story, they will tell it like someone is running around impersonating the electrician John Adams and, for some crazy reason, doing minor electrical work expertly. But when they tell that version, you can see in their faces they don't believe it.

April 24th

A QUARTER FOR KATIE

Katie Campbell was eight years old when she died. She had just learned to ride her bike and she was making large loops around the park at the top of Love Circle when a car came tearing up the road and into the park and, like a bubble bursting in the hot summer air, she was gone.

People see Katie all the time, right at the entrance to the park, and they have no idea she's a ghost. She looks just like a kid from the neighborhood, doing ordinary kid-from-the-neighborhood things. She looks happy.

But in the morning, that's different.

She's not there every morning, but often enough, right at the break of day, as the first rays of light cut across the horizon, she is sitting there in the middle of the street, her knees drawn up to her chin, and she is crying.

"I want my momma," she says, so plain it forces your heart into your throat, even before she looks up at you, the way kids do when they still have full faith in adults. "Please, can I borrow a quarter to call my momma?"

Very few people can stand to not give her a quarter, if they have one. But, it is said, once she touches it, she disappears, and the quarter clanks to the asphalt.

If you are at the top of Love Circle and you notice quarters just outside the entrance to the park, this is because it is considered especially good luck to leave quarters for Katie and especially terrible luck to remove them.

April 25th

THE UNFORTUNATE GHOST

Dr. Dalton is a heart surgeon at Vanderbilt. Until moving into his home at the end of Park Ridge Drive in the nicest part of town he could afford, he considered himself to be a man of science, exclusively. Yes, of course, he would have agreed that there was a certain artistry to his profession, but artistry rooted firmly in the rational world.

Life is for the living. When you're dead, you're dead. Simple as that.

So he was embarrassed just at that level to have to call the Davidson County Paranormal League. He asked them to please come in unmarked vehicles and not their distinctive black van with the lightning painted on it.

He was relieved when they asked him not to tell them anything about the history of the house. Their psychic, they said, would tell them everything they needed to know. He could just confirm it in the morning.

So he went out onto the sleeping porch and tried to sleep while they investigated.

In the morning, he had a preliminary meeting with the group. They were tired and, bless their hearts, though they were trying, they were having a hard time stifling their giggles.

"So," said the leader, "that's unfortunate." His sidekick began to snicker.

"What can I do? What did the psychic say?"

"Honestly, I'm not sure," the leader said. "Joanne just sensed something, something friendly, but going about its own business. She thinks it's been here longer than the house, even. Maybe a dog. Maybe a person. She can't tell."

Dr. Dalton sighed. "I have a dog. I certainly know

the smell of dog farts."

"Farts," one of them burst out. "Your ghost farts!"

"Let's keep it professional," the leader snapped.

"So, what can I do?"

"You've tried having a priest bless the place?"

"I'm an atheist."

"I don't think the Unitarians care about that. Maybe they could help you?"

"I can't have this getting out. I have patients who are Unitarians."

"Well, then, I guess you could just keep your radio or TV on all the time."

"Just learn to live with a farting ghost?"

"Yep, that's about all we can recommend."

April 26ᵗʰ

MASON'S RESTAURANT

It's pretty easy to be the youngest person in Mason's Restaurant by a couple of decades, even if you're in your 50s. Don't let this dissuade you from going, though.

Mason's is the kind of place where you can buy enough food to fill your whole table and pay ten dollars for it—eggs and bacon and toast and coffee and biscuits with or without gravy, maybe some ham, you want some sausage? Maybe some pancakes? French toast?

It's as good as Hermitage Cafe, but without the overnight hours and all the cops at the counter.

"Do y'all get famous people in here?" I asked one morning.

"Oh, sure," my waitress said. "Bill Monroe came in all the time before he died. And Lefty Frizzell..."

"Oh, kids today don't know who Lefty Frizzell is," one of the other waitresses said.

"I do too know who Lefty Frizzell is," I said, feeling a little indignant.

"He stops by every once in a while for breakfast," My waitress said. "You know, he's just down the road here."

"He's dead," I said.

"Oh, we all know that," she said. "But his money's good and he tips well, so we don't mind."

The other waitress came by. "She can speak for herself. It gives me the willies."

"Well, bless your heart, I hope you don't let on when he's here," my waitress said.

"Of course not," the other waitress scoffed. "Unlike some people, I am not rude."

83

"One time," my waitress motioned to the other gal, "I wouldn't let her husband come in and wait while we closed, fifteen years ago, and she still won't let me forget it."

LUCY WHITE

Lucy White was a woman so long ago she barely remembers it. She remembers the boards she put down on the floor of the shack so that she could cross from her bed to the fireplace without getting her feet wet when it rained and the water streamed through the low spot in the dirt floor. She remembers the smell of mash bubbling in the still. And she has a sense that she felt satisfied when she finally lay down under the dirt.

She remembers that her life was hard.

And she delights in how easy it is for the folks who live on her land now. She remembers the first indoor stove she saw, how she would open and shut the door, marveling at the luxury of not having to cook over an open fire. And now? Now she will turn on stovetops that don't even get hot unless you put a pan on them. And she will rummage around in people's cabinets, trying every pot.

She remembers trying to nurse her first baby, how afraid she was, how hard it was. And she will watch young mothers with their first babies and the luxuries of bottles and formula. She loves to help. She will coo over a fat baby. She will press the buttons on the microwave while you fish breast milk out of the freezer.

And don't even get her started on toilets. She will flush your toilet fifty times in a row, if she thinks it won't bother you too much.

She loved to watch them race horses down the Pike. And then bicycles, and now cars. She is always yelling, "Faster, faster, faster," though it's rare that anyone hears her.

For a long time after she was dead, she kept waiting for someone to show up and point her to where she was supposed to be. No one came. She thought maybe she'd been forgotten.

But now, she thinks, "Here I am, where I should be."

*April 28*th

Here, behind a low stone wall, down a little-traveled road, in back of a church on Trinity Lane, is Lock One Park. It goes without saying that there used to be a lock here on the Cumberland River. And before that, Eaton's Station, within sight of Fort Nashboro, which most folks, back in the day, called French Lick Station.

If you can get over the stone wall, the park slowly descends to the river, and throughout there are foundations of old buildings, old tracks, old paths, old walls.

If you feel inclined, go down about halfway to the river, just past where the path curves and the ruins switch from stone to brick. Sit there for a while. I can't tell you how long. Sometimes shutting your eyes helps.

You'll hear the noise from the nearby interstate and kids playing up at street level and birds, the constant chatter of birds. You might hear a mother calling for her child. Nothing strange about that, except the accent sounds so old-fashioned. And your wait is soon satisfied by the sound of children running past, delighted with a frog or a crawfish they found.

You might also hear the zip of the back and forth of saws on trees and men working to clear the timber from the hills. And there is the noise of the barge as it signals its approach to the lock. And there are the thwacks of arrows hitting wood. And there is the sound of the thunder of thousands of bison moving past you to wade through the shallows.

Still, wait for it. Do not yet open your eyes.

Give it long enough and you might hear a thud like a log falling to the ground, followed by another, and another, until you realize those are footsteps. The smell, also, will be a giveaway. Maybe, if you are lucky, there will be a whole herd.

Stay still. But open your eyes and see the mastodons come down to the river to drink, their ghosts still roaming the state in large herds, though this is the only surefire place to see them.

April 29ᵗʰ

THE DEVIL'S CURSED GOLD

It's well-known that the Devil has a summer home here in Nashville. So it didn't take too many Sundays before preachers were blaming him for the flood. The truth is that he had nothing to do with it. The Devil rarely does things, at least not anymore. Lately he's just been making suggestions or turning off alarm clocks, or whispering tiny doubts in people's ears.

It's not very hard, if you're the Devil, to do big acts of evil. But how small a wrong can he do and still have it spiral out of control? That's the question he's been lately trying to answer.

So he has been brushing his hand on the arms of lonely administrative assistants and smiling shyly at the married choir director. In office fights, he always picks the side of the woman who keeps a bottle of booze in her desk for when she's feeling like no one gets her, just to see if one person supporting her when no one else will makes it worse.

He is the crack in the sidewalk. The snag in your hose at a needed job interview.

After he got word his "second home" was flooding, he was a firefighter in chest-deep water rescuing people out of flooding apartments. This, honestly, was not so much about doing evil as preserving his ability to do evil. He had plans for some folks, and he had no interest in seeing them change their fates.

But he was also back in Nashville and in the water for another reason, and that reason did not bode well for Paul Turner.

Paul Turner was a history professor at Vanderbilt whose focus was the lives of free blacks in Nashville, prior to the Civil War. He was especially interested in Dr. Jack

89

Macon, who had been the slave of William Macon, but who earned his freedom and, due to the intervention of his patients, the right to stay in Tennessee even after being freed.

Turner had a theory that Dr. Jack, as he was called, was William's half-brother. He had nothing more than a hunch and the fact that William's father and son were both named John. But Turner had gone to the Tennessee State Library and Archives to see what he could learn.

There wasn't much. A mention in an early city directory. An entry in the interment records of the city cemetery. Already things he'd seen at the Nashville Library.

"Oh, this is interesting," the woman helping Turner said, as she came back to his table. "We actually have a file on William Macon. But it's only got one thing in it, and that seems to have to do with Jack Macon."

"What's that?" Turner said.

"It's a map. See? At the top here, it's faded, but doesn't that look like it says 'Property of Jack Macon'?"

"Hmm, and judging by the size of Nashville, I'd have to say this map was made probably right around the time that Jack got his freedom." Turner was already making notes.

The Macon map contained one odd feature. It showed a small pond on the east side of the river, just north of where the Navy Operational Support Center is, in the middle of what is now the golf course. And next to the pond, even closer to the current location of the old naval building, was an X. A faint X, but the kind of X that makes historians feel for a second like they're going to be able to call their friends in the archaeology department and tell them to suck it.

But what could Turner do? You can't just go around digging up a golf course.

Little did he know, the Devil was sitting right across

town thinking the same thing. Because it turns out that Turner and the Devil, though they did not know it, had complementary problems. Turner knew the location of whatever Macon had marked but not what it was. The Devil knew what it was, but not exactly where.

Yes, of course, he had someone whose job it was to trail Macon, but it turns out that a man didn't grow up to be one of the most powerful doctors in the state back in the 1850s without learning a thing or two about how to give a devil the slip. The Devil figured it was in the park, but he didn't know for certain.

Let us stop and imagine for a moment how easy it would have been for Turner to do the right thing. He could have published an article on the Macon map, could have done a couple of interviews with the local media, gotten some public excitement about his treasure hunt and gotten permission to excavate.

I hadn't considered it until just now, but maybe the Devil and Paul Turner met before this. Maybe the Devil was the lanky grad student with the black eyes, just at Vanderbilt for the day using the library. I mean, who uses the library anymore? And later, as Turner tried to awkwardly hit on him, maybe he hinted about discovering the map, about the X that marked a spot that seemed easy enough to find.

That would make sense of how the Devil and Turner ended up on the golf course the Monday after the flood. Turner had just walked in off of Sevier Street. The Devil, now a tattooed fireman with dimples, had commandeered a boat and come in through the flood water.

The Devil found Turner up to his waist in a hole.

"You find anything?" the Devil asked.

"Just now," Turner said, with a look of unmitigated delight on his face, so caught up in his discovery that he didn't even hide what he was up to. "I've about got it loose." The Devil jumped down in the hole with him and helped him rescue a wooden box, about the size of a small microwave, out of the mud. The Devil then lifted Turner out of the hole and Turner, in return, gave a hand to the Devil.

They both plopped to the ground, dirty and happy, with the box between them. Turner pulled out a knife and pried open the lid. The box was full of gold coins. Turner's first thought, not realizing who he was sitting next to, was that he could take the fireman, if he surprised him.

The Devil's first thought, interestingly enough, was whether he could get Turner to take the gold.

Just when it seemed like there might be a fixed fight, an old man came walking up. He was dressed very neatly in a faded black suit, wearing a top hat that seemed just a tad too formal for the circumstances. He had a cane, topped with a silver handle that he held more like a staff.

"That's my gold," the old man said, as if to end any discussion before it started.

"I assumed you had no more use for it," the Devil said.

"We had a deal," the old man said.

"You cheated," the Devil sputtered.

"Come now," the old man said. "We both know you got stupid and lazy during those years. Things were too easy for you and you got sloppy. That's not cheating. That's just smart."

"What kind of deal?" Turner asked.

"I said, 'You give me my family near me and the money to free them and once that money's spent, you can have me.' He said I seemed like the kind who might need a deal like that," Dr. Macon spoke with polite contempt.

"And you never spent the money," the Devil lamented.

"Not yet, anyway," Dr. Macon said, a smile hinting

at the corners of his mouth.

"Well, you can't spend it where you are now," the Devil said.

"Still, a deal is a deal," Dr. Macon said.

The Devil switched tactics. "Your map has been found. Certainly, you don't plan on standing around here all the time guarding this spot."

"No," Dr. Macon said, "I truly don't. So, mister, the gold's fate is your fate now. You guard it until I get back for it."

And before the Devil could even scream, Dr. Macon had tossed up his cane, grabbed the end of it and swung it like a bat, into Paul Turner's head. Turner was dead almost instantly.

"Are you kidding me?" the Devil sputtered, as Dr. Macon tossed the gold back into the hole.

"I'm starting to suspect that gold might be cursed for you," Dr. Macon said, smiling. "That's two souls it's lost you."

They say when it's rainy, the ghost of Paul Turner is often seen out there on the golf course, pacing around the spot where he died, muttering about his circumstances. Folks who've seen him say he's an omen of bad luck.

As for the Macon map, the State Library and Archives claims to not be able to find it anymore.

*April 30**th*

WE ARE OUR OWN GHOSTS

Minnie Robertson was eighty-two years old. Her great-grandson, who they all called Pinky, was just sixteen. He was sitting in the back of a police cruiser because he had obeyed when the police yelled, "Come out with your hands up."

Mrs. Robertson was sitting on the floor of what used to be her house, resting her head against the door frame of what used to be the entrance to her bedroom. It had been more than two months since the flood and the house was down to studs and the wooden subfloor. She still swore she could smell the creek water.

She dreamed of the little house on Delray Drive all the time. Not bad flood dreams, like some folks. Just dreams of ordinary days. Of walking from the kitchen to the front door. Of the tiny gold cross that hung by the bathroom mirror. Some nights, she would just dream she was sleeping in her own bed. Not memories, exactly, just her dreaming she was still in the old house.

After the flood waters had receded, she stood in her front yard and watched the volunteers tossing out dumpsters full of her ruined house. At first, she had tried to save photographs, and important papers, trying to separate them and dry them on the front lawn. But everything—the one photograph of her on her wedding day, the pictures of all her children and grandchildren and great-grandchildren—all were ruined beyond salvation.

"Just let me see," she said, on the second day. "Just let me go in and see." And she could stand it all, until she got to the small kitchen and saw the cupboard door under the sink peeling apart, the top layers curling away from the bottom layers.

How many times had her grandchildren opened and

95

shut that door, looking for pots to drum on or places to play?

She didn't want to interrupt the volunteers after that. So she would drive over from Geneva's house in the middle of the night and climb the front steps, as she had always done, and she would wander her empty house, in the dark, until she felt calm again.

The neighbors were never going to call the police, she thought. If there were any folks left on her block, surely they would understand. And the people the next block over did not want the attention of the authorities. And there was no one behind her; just the creek, already back in its banks.

She had not figured on the sightseers who found themselves driving aimlessly through the empty streets, trying to make sense of what happened. And when they saw a figure moving so deftly through a house that was supposed to be empty, they figured someone was stealing the copper pipes and they did call the police.

After that, she was forbidden to drive. That's how Pinky came to be involved. He often stayed with his grandmother when he was trying to stay off his stepfather's radar. And, because he was on the couch frequently when Mrs. Robertson was sneaking out at night, he knew long before the police were involved that she had been going somewhere.

So he was not surprised when she came to him one night and said, "I've been thinking. There might be something in the attic. We should go look and see if anything got saved in the attic."

"Gran," he said, "you know we can't do that." But of course he couldn't turn her down.

So off they went in his car, in the middle of the night, when no one was around. He thought to bring flashlights, so he took one up the ladder and she took one and wandered around her small house.

It was the doorway to her bedroom that broke her

heart, after all this time. There, in faded pencil marks, were all the heights of all her grandchildren and great grandchildren, including the one now rummaging around in the attic.

"Everything's gone," she said quietly, "But this stays? Lost every single dish, but pencil marks don't wash away?" And so she sat down in the doorway and leaned up against those marks, as if she could, by proximity, get back to the moments they were made.

"I found something," Pinky said, as he came back down the ladder. "I found this." He handed her a picture of a stern-looking girl his age.

"That was me," Mrs. Robertson said. "That was when I first went to work for Mrs. Bradley. Her husband had bought her a camera on one of his trips to New York. She was always taking pictures of everyone. This is the first one she took of me. I got used to it after a while. Smiled more."

"I only found this one," he said.

"That's too bad," she said. "I would have liked for you to have had one of me smiling."

"Oh, no, Gran," he said, "I can't take this." He blurted out this next part. "Are you dying?"

"A little every day," she said, still leaning against the door frame. "Listen," she said, grabbing at his jeans. "We are from the past. Me from longer ago than you. And we haunt the present, wandering around trying to make sense of how things are now. We're the ones who need explaining. We're the ones who are lost and who need saved. We're our own ghosts. That's what I want you to know."

"I don't even know what that means," he said, but he kept repeating it, even later, in the squad car, because he didn't want to ever forget it.

First thing the next morning, when the officer who

took the call was getting off his shift, he had to wait in his car for his shaking sobs to pass before he could go into the station. He cried about that ancient woman, sitting on the floor of her condemned house, talking about how she was a ghost now. And he cried for himself, that he had to see things like that and couldn't help.

October

October 1st

"I still dream I am drowning," she said to me. "Some mornings I wake up and I can't catch my breath, can't make my lungs take in air again.

"I can't stand it. I still see water everywhere, how the bottoms of trees are still so dirty, even with all of this rain. And I see that other people don't see it. I feel like I'm seeing a ghost. The empty shells of houses, the garbage still caught in fences. Everywhere I look is the ghost of water. How can they not see it?"

I had come to ask her about another ghost, a particular Alabaman who seems to haunt all over town and with whom it was rumored she'd had a particularly strange run-in, but this is what she wanted to talk about, for the little bit that she wanted to talk. She then bowed her head at her dressing table and squeezed her eyes shut. It felt so private that I almost turned away.

And then she sat up straight, wiped each eye with just the edge of her finger, and then followed that with the blotting of a tissue.

"Well," she said, "No one came to see me being a big ol' baby about this." And so she stared in the mirror, fussing with her hair, trying on two or three different smiles, and finally sliding into her sequined jacket.

And just like that, she was the singer, grateful and delighted to be performing for her audience, as if she had no care in the world but how to best entertain you. I was struck by the thought of all the women in this city who have steeled themselves by swallowing their grief, as if showing you a sweet face no matter the circumstances was the bodily equivalent of "Bless your heart."

It was an act designed to wither you, if you knew

how to read it, but also one they could perform in public and never be taken as rude by the clueless people they meant it toward.

The singer went over to the door frame with an old tube of lipstick and made a mark right at chin level, like you would to measure the growth of a child.

"I know," she said. "We're all supposed to be over it by now. But I still need this."

"What is that?" I asked.

"That's how high the water came up in my house. There's not a place I go now I don't leave the water's mark."

October 2ⁿᵈ

RACHEL JACKSON

I don't know if this story is true, but I love it so much that I hope it is. Rachel Jackson was a Donelson by birth, daughter of John Donelson, one of the founders of Nashville. There are Donelsons all over the place and few of them rest easily. Rachel, though, is the ghost of this story.

Perhaps it starts, like most good hauntings do, while she was still alive. She was, it seems, the kind of woman your grandfather might have called a real dame, a broad, and meant it as a compliment. She was an accidental bigamist and smoked a corn-cob pipe. She seemed to have a real lust for life and was, I suspect, a bit of a trouble-maker.

Anyway, her home, The Hermitage, is run by The Ladies' Hermitage Association, who do and have done wonderful work preserving and maintaining the home and the grounds.

But here's the deal as I heard it, from a person who has sworn me to secrecy. Supposedly, there are two portraits of Rachel Jackson in the house—a portrait of her as a young, beautiful woman, which hangs where everyone can see it, and a portrait of her in her older, plumper years, which does not. And, supposedly, the portrait of the older Rachel Jackson was discovered in a very odd manner.

One day, a couple of members of The Ladies' Hermitage Association were changing the sheets on Andrew Jackson's bed when one of them lifted up the mattress and discovered the portrait hidden there. Not knowing what to do with it, they stuck it in the back of a wardrobe. The women didn't think to mention the portrait, assuming that it had been deliberately placed by another member under the mattress at some point, and that, if anyone had needed it for something, she would have said. After all, how could a portrait lie under a mattress unknown and undiscovered all

103

this time?

But no, when they finally did mention it, no one knew anything about a portrait. So they all promptly rush into the bedroom, retrieved the portrait, and examined it. They are certain it's a portrait of her that has until now been unknown.

But there was a problem.

"She's fat," said one member. And it was agreed that if the public is going to have an idea of Rachel Jackson, it's best that it be of a young, healthy, thin Rachel, not one who is old and fat.

And so the portrait was put in the attic, never to be seen again.

At least, that was the intention.

But the rumor is that apparently Mrs. Jackson didn't appreciate the idea that her old, fat self wasn't good enough for public consumption. And so it is said that, even though every tour guide is told to walk the house once in the morning, before tours start, looking for anything that might be out of place, and once in the evening after tours are over, again looking for anything that might be out of place, that portrait won't stay in the attic.

Sometimes they'll find it in the middle of the day, propped up in a chair. Sometimes on the bed. Sometimes leaning against the wall in the front hall, like someone meant to hang it right by the entrance, but left for a moment, in search of a hammer and some nails.

October 3ʳᵈ

THE THREE BABIES

It was not that long ago that they were looking to widen Hillsboro Pike where it crosses Old Hickory Boulevard, down there by the big church. And you may recall that they found an ancient grave site there, and the bodies of three babies.

These babies were so old they had no people left—not just in the area, but at all. Words like Cherokee, Chickasaw, and Muskogee are too new to mean anything to those babies. And yet it is those folks who came to watch out for the babies, to fight against them being moved and to fight against their graves being desecrated.

There were lawsuits and protests and flags and ribbons tied to trees and poles as if to say, "These babies mattered. They still matter."

There are two houses of worship there, and I will not tell you which one did right and which did wrong. I will just say that one of them could have given up some parking space so that the road could go through and leave the babies undisturbed, but they did not. The other one offered parking to the protesters and cookies and lemonade.

The babies are under the road now.

And I hear that at night you can hear the laughter of small children, and speech in a language no one knows anymore. And I hear that folks at one house of worship, when they hear it, rush to their cars and cling tightly to their keys, to keep their shaking hands from dropping them. And at the other house of worship, when they hear the same noise, the folks nod to each other sadly, and sometimes one of them will walk toward the intersection, singing soft lullabies, to help the dead sleep.

*October 4*th

SMALL ROCKS

Here is a sad story I heard. There is a son, who is old now, whose mother died when he was young. They lived out in the country, down Bull Run Road, and she was buried in their family plot. Every Sunday he can, he still goes out to her grave and sits with her. He then leaves something— a small rock, a penny, his receipt from lunch—just a little something to let her know he's still there.

And there is a mother, who died when her son was still young, who rises early every Sunday morning, and walks from the cemetery to the old farmhouse where her son still lives and she leaves on his doorstep something—a small rock, a twisted root, a fine layer of dirt, the feather from a molting bird, an earthworm. And she sits in the rocker on the front porch all Sunday morning, just trying to spend some time with her son.

Neither knows of the other's habit.

Only the small neighbor girl knows this. If she isn't forced to go to church, she will run through the cow pasture and hide herself behind the old stone wall. She peeks over to watch the two of them pass right through each other.

"When I'm a grown-up," she says to herself later, in her room, "I will tell them."

But when she is grown, she convinces herself that she imagined them.

October 5ᵗʰ

EL PROTECTOR

My friend John asked me about "El Protector" over lunch one day, asked if I'd heard anything about it. At the time, there was a big police initiative to reach out to the Hispanic community called "El Protector," which we considered to be something of a sad joke. 'Yes, we're trying to deport your friends and family, but we also want to work with you to reduce crime in your area, so please, call us.'

As you might imagine, this didn't work so well.

"No, not the police thing," he clarified. "That thing on Charlotte."

Well, this is how it works in Nashville, often. Everyone who didn't speak English who lived or worked along Charlotte Pike knew about El Protector. I didn't know anyone who spoke English as his first language, except for John, who had heard of it.

John has a friend, Joselito, who agreed to have beers with us at the Las Palmas on Charlotte. And I asked him about El Protector. He laughed and said what I had said. "Who wants to call the police? They'll just take away your friends and the problems are left behind. Better to stick with your friends and take care of the problems yourselves."

"No, John, explain to him."

And so John explained to him.

"Oh. That's nothing. Just stories."

"Yes, but I want to know the stories."

He turned to John and they had a long conversation.

John then turned to me. "He says it's nothing. Swamp gas rising out of the creek and then up the hill toward the KFC and that there's a scientific explanation for it."

"Wait. He's saying there's a light that rises up out of the creek and heads west along the street?"

I waited for more discussion.

"He's saying that's not what people say, but that's the most likely explanation."

"What *do* people say?"

"I can tell you," our waiter said, dropping off another round of beers and some more corn chips. "It is a man with a lantern. You can see the light from a long way away, clear down by Bobbie's Dairy Dip and it comes…"

"No, it comes too fast to be a man," interjected another waiter.

"A man on a horse?"

"Oh, yes, a man on a horse."

"It comes, just the light—this faint yellow light—down the road and you hurry to get in your car or back in the building. You don't want to be out when it gets by you."

"Or it will throw its giant pumpkin head at you?" I joked.

"No, no. If you are good, probably nothing. But, if you are bad, you will die."

"Wait, El Protector kills people?" I tried to clarify.

"A ghost can't kill people," John said, in a way that seems designed to end the conversation.

"Of course not," Joselito said.

"Someone else kills you," the waiter said. "Seeing El Protector up close is a curse."

"How often does this happen?"

"Oh, all the time," the other waiter said. "You can sit in our parking lot all night and you will see it."

110

"Because I'll be hallucinating from lack of sleep," said John.

And we all laughed, and that's the end of it.

Except, of course, it's not.

A couple of months later I'm having lunch with John again and he seems very shaken, but he won't say much, except to tell me about how his kids are doing in school.

"No, really. What's troubling you?"

"I saw it."

"What? The light? The ghost? Up close?"

"JJ was sick and it was the middle of the night, and I had to run to Walmart and you know how they're closing down 40 at night to do repaving? So I was coming back home up Charlotte when I saw a light coming toward me. I thought at first it was a motorcycle. But it was going too slow. And the light seemed too high up. It was just like they said. Like where a lantern would be if you were holding it out in front of you on horseback. And..."

"Did you see it? Did you see it up close?"

"No. I chickened out. When it got close enough, I shut my eyes."

"While you were driving?"

"I hit a dog. Killed it. It was terrible. I feel terrible."

"Maybe it was an evil dog."

"Oh, God, shut up."

October 6*th*

A DYING FIRE

One of the lovely things about Nashville are the times in autumn when it is warm and sunny all day long, but just cool enough at night that a fire in the evening will warm the whole house all night. Maggie Wilson, who had just turned ten, was staying with her grandparents out in Donelson. For the most part, she was bored.

If she complained, her granny would put a dustcloth or a broom in her hand and she'd be set to doing chores. If she just kept quiet and out of the way, she might spend a whole Saturday afternoon hidden under an old magnolia reading, or watching inchworms in the garden.

In the evenings, she would help her Paw Paw build a fire in the big old brick fireplace in the living room. He always aimed to for a one-match fire, but rarely did they achieve it.

Once the fire was going, though, Maggie would spend all evening, she and the dog, just watching the flames dance and the embers glow.

One evening, as the fire was dying down, Maggie thought she saw a face in the red coals. She closed her eyes, in a long blink, then opened one, then the other, to try to see if it was a trick of the light.

She was not sure.

"Granny?" she turned to get her grandmother's opinion, but her grandmother, a Duratt before she was married, was already asleep in the recliner.

When Maggie turned back to the flames, the face was gone.

It was a few weeks before she saw the face again, though this time it seemed more defined, more clearly a man with a rugged face. This time she poked the coals with the fire poker and they fell apart, taking the illusion with them.

After that she thought she caught glimpses of him quite often, not just a face, but she would swear she saw a whole tiny figure sometimes, moving.

Even still, she had often been told she "had an active imagination," and so she figured that she was just actively imagining it.

And then, one day, she saw the face take form, almost human-size, and the coal-red eyes opened, and the coal-red mouth opened and the man said something. She leaned in to try to hear, and her Paw Paw startled and yelled, "Maggie Wilson! Get your head out of that fire."

When Maggie's dad got home on leave, she babbled at him nonstop for at least two hours—from the airport to the house, through dinner, and even while her ice cream melted on the spoon.

"And the man in the fire wants to talk to me," she said. Her father and grandparents had, until that sentence, been politely and somewhat delightedly tuning her out. It was good to spend time with each other and good to not have to come up with anything to say right away. The mention of the man in the fire caught their attention.

"What's that, honey?" her dad said.

"The man in the fire. He's always talking to me."

Her dad took a long time to ask his next question. "And what's he say?"

"I don't know," she said, thoughtfully, "I can barely hear him. He's so quiet. But I think he wants me to help him out."

"Out?" her grandmother said. "Help him out or help him get out?"

"I don't know," she said with a shrug. A look passed

among the three adults, over Maggie's head and beyond her notice.

There were no fires until after her father was gone again. But one night, during the dark of the moon, Granny Wilson sat Maggie down in front of a dying fire and said, "Tell me when you see him."

They waited, but not so long as you'd think, and there he was—first a small figure running through a glowing fiery forest. Then, after a shift of logs, a full face, his mouth moving.

"Granny! Granny!" Maggie said, "Here he is!"

And her Granny leaned over, sprinkling first a fistful of salt into the embers and following it up with the remnants of her tea. She spoke something softly—*Laissez-la tranquille*—and the fire went out.

"A dying fire is the Devil's doorway," she said to Maggie.

The next day, her grandfather bricked up the fireplace.

October 7ᵗʰ

STILL HAUNTED

Not that long ago, but back when we all took for granted that we did not live in a river, Daniel Forte stole a long leg bone out of the bluff at the bottom of Bells Bend.

He had been fishing off of the end of the boat ramp, when he decided that the small shore just downstream, littered with white shells, was a better prospect, since there was a large, upended tree in the shallow water there.

He had to wade through the river to get there, but the Cumberland was so calm he barely felt it tug on the legs of his jeans as he skirted along the bottom of bluff to the tiny beach. Maybe twenty steps, maybe fewer.

He found the bone almost immediately. He was grabbing onto bare roots for balance and, as he stepped onto the shore, he put his hand out to steady himself. When he touched the bluff, he touched bone.

Maybe it had already been raining that spring and we just thought nothing of it. Maybe when something wants to be found you can't escape the misfortune of finding it. Either way, he pressed his fingers into the mud, grabbed hold of it, gave it a slight yank and out it popped, with surprisingly little effort. A whole thigh bone.

He squatted down and washed it in the river so clear, watching as the mud slowly swirled away and off downstream.

When he went to go home, he tossed it in the passenger side of his truck. He wasn't even as far as the Ashland City Highway when he thought he saw a man out of the corner of his eye, sitting shotgun. Forte almost died right then, swerving off the road like he did.

A few days later, he asked his girlfriend what she'd done with the bone from his truck. He was going to take it

117

down to the bar, show it to a few of the guys, see what they thought.

"I gave it to the dog," she said.

Before he could even think to be mad, he was running through the house and out the back door. The bone sat under the catalpa tree. The dog stood nearby, its chain stretched taut, staring at something.

"Come on, boy," Forte said, but the dog would not take its eyes off the spot under the tree where the bone sat. Forte walked over and grabbed the bone. The dog—his dog—lunged at him, barking and growling and snapping.

"What's going on?" his girlfriend asked.

"Dog's fucked up, I guess," he said with a shrug.

During the flood, Daniel Forte was out of town. He was over in Missouri helping his cousin move. He called home a couple of times, but his girlfriend never answered. He didn't think much of it.

I don't know what he thought about on the drive home, as he passed swollen creeks turned into rivers; as he detoured around washed-out roads. I do know that by the time he got to Nashville, he was afraid.

He couldn't get to his house. He parked at the end of the street and walked to the police tape and watched, along with a small crowd, as rescuers launched boats off the low point in the road.

"The dog's dead," was the first thing his girlfriend told him, when he finally found her. "Water rose so fast, and I couldn't get out to him." He waited for her to say what she always said, that he shouldn't leave the dog tied up out back. But she seemed uninterested in blaming him.

"How did you get out?" he asked.

"I heard something," she said, "a voice or a laugh or..." again, she lost interest in trying to explain. "I just got out. I waited on the roof. They came and got me." After a long while, she said, "Here," and handed him the bone.

"Do you think this was it? Do you think I did this?" He asked, but she said nothing.

For the next few weeks she was like a ghost, walking around the hotel room like she had lost track of what anchored her here. Forte wondered if she might fade completely away.

One Sunday, he took the bone and went back down to the end of Old Hickory Boulevard, deep in Bells Bend. The water in the Cumberland was still high and brown and fast moving. He slipped going down the boat ramp, but righted himself. The shore was smaller, mostly underwater, and so it was farther—thirty steps, certainly, maybe more. And from the moment he stepped into the river it pulled at him, swirled around him, and brushed brown mud and sticks against him.

When he stepped onto the shore, it sucked him in. Without thinking, he pulled back, trying to get his foot out of the mire. He struggled to regain his balance and, at the last second, pitched himself forward. He fell into the mud. The bone rolled out of his grasp, toward the water. He grabbed after it, stopping it before it went into the river.

He stood with some difficulty in the shin-deep mire. The driest spot was nearest the bluff, so he struggled over to a small patch of firm ground. He dug into the side of the bluff as best he could and put the bone back.

He waited to see if something would shift; if he would feel that something had been righted.

He felt nothing.

He ended up having to scramble back up the bluff just to get out. And I'll be damned if he had driven barely to the Ashland City Highway when he saw, out of the corner of his eye, a man riding shotgun.

October 8th

THE GOODLETTSVILLE GAL

They say there's a gal in Goodlettsville who can speak to the dead as easily as I might pick up the phone and speak to you. She is young, maybe nineteen or twenty, and lives out in a hollow along Brick Church Pike. They say everything in her house must be brand-new, because anything even remotely associated with a dead person will bring her into communication with the dearly departed, like a radio you can't turn off.

They say she helps police from around the country solve crimes.

Almost none of this is true. I have, by now, talked to enough police officers that I felt like I could press them about whether Metro had ever worked with the Goodlettsville Gal.

Finally, one of them shook her head and asked me, "You know what it means when a police department admits to working with a psychic?'"

"Instant loss of credibility?" I guessed.

She laughed and explained, "No, it means we either have a good idea but can't prove it, so we're tossing the 'psychic' information out there as a way of shaking the bushes, or it means we've got something through less-than-legal means and we need a way to 'discover' it again in a way that will stand up in court." She paused, and her face turned more serious. "Think of some of the high-profile cases that we have not solved. You think if we had a workable psychic, those families wouldn't have some answers?"

"So, you think the Goodlettsville Gal is just a myth?"

"Oh, no. I did not say that," she said, stretching out every word just a little more than usual.

The officer wrote down an address on a napkin, slid

it across the table to me and looked at me as if I had no idea what I was asking.

"Why don't you go see? I heard she's up to something this afternoon, in fact."

So off I went, with nothing more than that address. No name, no phone number, just a sense that there was something strange worth seeing and if I hurried, I could catch it.

She was waiting at the end of the driveway when I got there. She was small and had hair in that no-color state between the towhead of childhood and the dark brown of adult, which she wore pulled back in a ponytail.

"If you want to hang out a little bit," she said, pointing me to where I could park in the front yard, "some Skagges are on their way, and I'm going to do my thing for them. You're welcome to watch."

The Skaggs family claims to have been here since their ancestor, Henry Skaggs, came into the area with Kasper Mansker in 1771. Interestingly enough, some Skaggses believe they are cursed, following from an incident in which they believe Henry witnessed Mansker killing an Indian, the first such incident in Middle Tennessee, though, certainly not the last.

There's much contention about both of these facts. Henry Skaggs, many say, was back in Virginia when the incident occurred, thus meaning Skaggses have not been here continuously since then (though folks will concede Skaggses certainly returned at some point shortly after) and that Henry could not have been cursed for his witnessing a murder he did not prevent, since he wasn't there to witness it.

And don't even get the Skaggses started on whether there is a curse. The fact is that some believe it and some don't, and they all have made themselves somewhat amateur historians and genealogists in an effort to bolster their particular claims.

It was this tendency for historical sleuthing that brought this branch of the Skaggs family to the Goodlettsville Gal this particular afternoon. Their grandfather, a man in his late 80s, was preparing to die. Not right away, but just wanting to settle things on earth before stepping off into whatever comes next.

Not normally an affectionate man, he had taken to making a point of telling his son that he loved him and making sure that his daughters knew how proud he was of them. And he wanted to know what had happened to his sister, Maggie, who had taken off for school one day when she was 16 and never come home.

Some family members thought she'd probably just run off, but Big Daddy Skaggs refused to believe she would have left without telling him. He believed she was dead; that she had been all this time. He just wanted to know for sure and to have the family record set straight before he died. The family conceded it was probably far too late to have the police look into it. After seventy years, what could there be to find?

But they thought the Goodlettsville Gal could help.

And so, here they were, Big Daddy; his son, called, of course, Little Daddy; and Bill and Sharon, who, though also parents, were just called "Bill and Sharon." If Big Daddy or Little Daddy were called anything else, I didn't hear it. They sat around the Goodlettsville Gal's parents' dining room table. The Goodlettsville Gal sat at the head. I stood in the doorway between the kitchen and the dining room.

Though it was sunny out, when I turned out the lights, the room felt like late evening.

The Gal asked Big Daddy, as she lit the candle in the center of the table, "Is there a song she liked? Or a song that you liked from back then? Something you could sing for me?"

Little Daddy said, "He's not much of a singer."

123

"That's all right," the Gal said, reaching out and patting Big Daddy on the arm. "That's just fine."

Big Daddy gave an embarrassed smile, but he began to sing "Sweet Leilani." Either nobody else knew it or they were reluctant to sing along, but Big Daddy had a fine voice, soft and low, cracking a little, but he took the song slow and sweet.

As he sang, the Gal shut her eyes and began to rock with the rhythm of Big Daddy's voice. And then, as she got a sense of the words, she too began to sing. Something in the room shifted, as if we were all suddenly drunk or dizzy. Everyone reached to steady themselves. The door behind me slowly swung shut. Then the door from the dining room to the front room. The chandelier over the table started to swing back and forth.

The Gal stood up and climbed onto the table. She grabbed hold of the swinging light fixture and reached for Big Daddy's hand. "Keep singing," she directed.

He did.

And she slowly turned toward the window, so her back was to us. And she said, in a loud voice, "Here we are! Open that gate. Come on out and tell me what I want to know." A cloud crossed the sun and the whole room seemed to shrink. Suddenly she twirled on her knees, almost knocking the candles over, and she looked right at Bill.

"You could die, you know. If you don't get a handle on your drinking, your grandfather will outlive you."

She then turned to Little Daddy, which meant that I could more clearly see her face. Somehow it looked as if someone older was behind her face. I don't know how to explain it better than that. It was as if an old woman was wearing a young girl as a mask. She studied him intently and finally said, "Yes. Yes, you did."

He bolted up from the table and paced in front of me, running his hands through his hair.

124

"Okay, okay," he whispered to himself. "I thought so."

Finally, she turned to Big Daddy. She looked him up and down and then she looked out into the sunny yard.

She said, "Your sister is at home. She says to tell you that you did kill her killer."

And then it was almost as if someone let the air out of the room. The gal from Goodlettsville sank to the table, her face resembling herself once again. The doors popped back open, as if a breeze had come rushing out of the room. And the room flooded with light as the sun came out from behind the cloud.

Most of the Skaggses were visibly shaken. Big Daddy, though, slumped like he'd just set down a heavy load. He opened up his wallet and counted out twenty-five twenty dollar bills.

"All right then," he said. "All right."

October 9ᵗʰ

Chuck Anderson lived through this. I should say that up front. He was young, six or seven, and his brother Antwane was twelve or thirteen. Their mother worked at the grocery store across from the projects there on Murfreesboro Road, just past where it changes names from Lafayette. The three of them lived in one of those low brick buildings that look more like barracks than homes and Antwane was charged with watching his brother after school, making sure they got next door to Mrs. Alexander's for dinner, and that after dinner they did their homework before watching TV.

This had worked well, without incident, for years. Not many, though longer than their mother could bear.

"Don't answer the door for no one," she said. "Don't play outside unless Mrs. Alexander is watching. And don't be hanging out with those boys on the corner."

They never did. They were good kids.

They were boys, though, and they horsed around. And one day they were chasing each other across the couch, and then leaping from the couch into the chair, and then onto the pillows stretched out across the floor, stepping stones across the hot lava. Around and around, at least a half a dozen times successfully, and then Chuck lost his footing jumping from the couch to the chair, and he slipped, and hit his head on the arm of the sofa, and fell, limp, to the ground.

Antwane stopped immediately and ran to his brother. He yelled for help. He ran outside. He knocked on Mrs. Alexander's door. Nothing. He ran back inside. Frantic, he died 9-1-1.

Long, long rings. Finally, an answer. "My brother's been hurt. Please, send help. My mom's at work. It's really bad."

"What's your address, son?"

And he gives it. And there is a long, long pause.

"How far in are you?"

Antwane can't understand what he's hearing. "I'm in the kitchen. My brother's in the living room."

Another long pause.

"Can you carry him?"

"I think so."

"Okay. You need to lift him up and carry him to Murfreesboro Road. The ambulance will meet you there."

"Okay."

So, he does. It takes him ten minutes at the most. So when the ambulance is not there, he doesn't think anything of it at first. But it doesn't come.

And it still doesn't come.

And Antwane by now is crying, and he's waving his arms at the passing cars, begging, "Stop, please stop. My brother ... hospital ..."

But no one stops.

Finally, one of the boys from the corner comes over to see what's going on. He yells at someone to get a car, and they load Chuck into the back seat and take him to the emergency room. One of them even goes back and gets Antwane's mom.

And like I said, Chuck is fine. He lives up around the corner from me and has some tech job I don't understand that lets him afford a big house with a nice yard. His mom lives up in Springfield with her sister.

Antwane died a while back, of cancer, but before that he was an accountant.

Here's why Chuck will not drive down Murfreesboro Road. Because sometimes a young boy, twelve or thirteen, will dart into traffic waving his hands, begging cars to stop. The look of terror on his face scares most of them, and they roll up their windows and speed up. Once or twice a year, though, a person will stop and the back door will open, and two young children will get into the back seat. But by the time the car gets past Purity Dairy, the driver will find the back seat is empty.

"I know why he's there," Chuck tells me one night, over beers. "He never could let go of it. He'd say, 'If I had a gun, I could have made someone stop,' or 'If I were white...' no offense... 'If I were white, someone would have stopped for a couple of white kids if one of them was hurt.' Hell, if we were white we wouldn't have even been living in that place. I know why he can't get past that. It makes sense to me.

"But they always see two kids. What am *I* doing there?"

October 10th

SOME GHOSTS MAKE YOU BLUSH

If you've ever been into any of the four-story buildings on Lower Broad or Second Avenue, you might find yourself wondering why, no matter what time of day it is, the music is always so loud.

You're not trying to be a party-pooper, you think, but how is a man supposed to talk to his wife over lunch with all that racket?

The racket is for a reason.

See, during the Civil War, this part of Nashville was basically a shopping mall of brothels. Every building housed prostitutes. And I'm not going to lie to you and tell you some romantic story about how wonderful it was. It was, in general, pretty terrible, and a pretty horrible way to make a living.

But it was a living, at a time when a lot of folks were starving.

Yes, women were treated poorly. Yes, they had diseases. Yes, oftentimes they lay there and stared at the slow shadows on the wall passing while they waited for the soldiers to be done with them. And sometimes they were beaten and robbed and killed, and no one cared.

Yes, all of that. But...

If you go into those restaurants, the ones that admit to being haunted, they will tell you some sad tale of women who, a hundred and fifty years on, still mope around and have nothing better to do than to rearrange furniture and silverware.

But the truth is that when it's quiet, bartenders will hear a woman clearing her throat at the end of the bar, the universal signal for "Pour me another one." When it's quiet, they can hear the silverware being pushed off the tables, as if someone has taken her arm and brushed it all aside in one dramatic motion, to make room for her butt or her hands and knees up there. When it's quiet, you can hear the moans of dead women—the gasps, the shrieks, the screams—and those places, all trying to be respectable now, can only wish those noises sounded scary.

October 11th

There are two great mysteries when it comes to the Opryland complex just off Briley. One is large and I cannot answer it: why did it seem like a good idea to close down Opryland and put up a mall? Could a mall and an amusement park not have worked hand-in-hand? I take comfort in knowing that everyone who works at Gaylord is haunted by this same question.

The other is smaller: why would you ever pay to park at the hotel when you can park at the mall for free and walk over?

That I have an answer for.

Because some folks do. You go to the movie theater side of the mall, park way out at the end of the parking lot, and then it's just a short walk over to a back entrance to the hotel.

But it's not exactly a nice walk. You are literally walking over the corpse of Opryland. There's an old gate, old sidewalks, old light fixtures and, to your left, the old cave that featured prominently in the Grizzly River Rampage, a water ride in which you and eleven others were seated in a round, barrel-like contraption and set off down a fake river, to get wet.

And sure, if you're filled with nostalgia for your Nashville childhood, it's kind of heartbreaking.

But what keeps people out is that you're walking along in broad daylight, and you can see your car behind you if you turn and look, and if you crane your neck you can see the hotel in front of you.

And there, on the path coming toward you, looking suitably tired and excited after a day's outing, is a family of four. At first, nothing at all about them seems that weird.

133

And then you realize that the parents are both smoking, and you can't remember the last time you saw people looking so at ease smoking in public. Or those shorts that the father and son are wearing. Sure, fashions come back, but shorts that short on men?

It's disconcerting. To the point where maybe it's just easier to pay the parking fee.

And I imagine that, as fashions continue to change and it becomes less and less easy to convince yourself that those could be people from your time, paying for parking becomes easier and easier to justify.

October 12th

There used to be a house on Old Glenrose, just across the train tracks from the big field behind Woodbine Baptist Church. If you have seen this field in the summer, it's hard to forget it, since there seems to be fifty sweaty men playing soccer in it at any given time. Men who are stripping off shirts with pinprick holes where their nametags go. Other men are switching from dress shoes to sneakers as fast as they can in their cars. Some of the men sometimes reach unconsciously to cover tattoos they're not sure they want the other men to see.

Where else can you see such a wide mix of men all enjoying the day?

You used to be able to sit on the porch of the house on Old Glenrose and watch them. When Laura was first born, before her mother had to go back to work, her mother would stand on the porch, a towel over her shoulder and then Laura draped over the towel, and her mother would pat her back and watch the men. Her mother had this fantasy, which she told no one, of one day going over there in her sneakers and shorts, and she imagined how all the men would laugh and tell her to go home, or frown and tell her that this was no place for a woman, but then she would somehow get the ball.

And just like they could be on that field and it didn't matter if they were lawyers or gang members or dishwashers or what, it wouldn't matter who she was—when she was on the field, she would be a player.

Laura grew up in the little house on Old Glenrose until she was four, when it burned down.

The fire spread quickly, and Laura's mother and father nearly died. Laura did die.

The firefighter who carried her out said only one

thing about it, ever, to anyone. One day, when he was sitting on his riding lawnmower, not moving, his wife came out to check on him. He turned to her, and said, "She should have had a whole life."

Her parents were still at Vanderbilt when the first 9-1-1 call came.

"9-1-1. What's your emergency?"

"Hay un fuego."

"Darlene, I've got a little kid speaking Spanish. Can you take it?"

Darlene got on the line while the other operator worked frantically to try to figure out where the little girl was calling from.

"Ola. ¿Qué dijo usted?"

"Mi mama está dormida."

And then nothing. The line went dead.

"What did she say to you?"

"En fuego? That's fire, right?"

"What's that address? Did we get the address? Dispatch, we've got to get trucks to the 700 block of Old Glenrose Avenue. 712 Old Glenrose Avenue."

There is nothing worse, you can imagine, than getting a 9-1-1 call from a child who is obviously in trouble, whether she knows it or not. And so the 9-1-1 operators sat for the next twenty minutes, checking the clock and waiting to hear something—anything—from 712 Old Glenrose Avenue.

After about a half an hour, their supervisor came in.

"We're going to need the tape of that Old Glenrose Avenue call."

"Oh, God, did someone die?"

136

"Yeah, two weeks ago. That house is burnt to the ground. Don't worry. Probably just some asshole kids gave that address just because."

"No, that's the address the system gave us. That's the house that call came from."

"Well, it must be a glitch in the system, then, because there's no house there anymore."

Of course they checked for glitches. Even sent an AT&T crew out there. But nothing.

And still the calls come. Not very often, but often enough that every operator is warned about them. And folks have quit after taking them.

"Here's what you've got to understand," Darlene said to me. "This isn't an easy job as it is. You're hearing people at some of the absolute worst moments of their lives, either because it's happening to them or because they're seeing something terrible happen to someone else, but you know you're sending help. You know you can send someone to help. No, it don't always work out, but at least there's something you can do.

"Who can you send to that poor little girl?"

October 13ᵗʰ

THE STRANGE CASE OF GEORGE HARDING

George Harding was a young man who fell into the Harpeth when it was swollen one spring and, though he was a strong swimmer, he went under and never came up. Though there is a marker for him in the graveyard by the Ensworth School, his body was not recovered until recently. He was found by Jim Sharp while he and his son were walking along the Harpeth in the small park under the Route 100 bridge. The flood had, apparently, uncovered the bones that had been buried in the bank.

Sharp, upon discovering the bones, immediately called the police, who came out and marked off the area as a crime scene. They took a statement from Sharp, and he and his son headed for their nearby home.

Everything was fine until Sharp got out of the car. Even before he could get around to open his son's door, he felt what he later described as a hard wind.

"I felt," he told me, "like I had been punched in the face from the inside. Especially, right along my nose and under my eyes. I felt this enormous pressure.

"And then I was seeing double. I mean, it was like seeing double or wearing bifocals or something. Except, if I looked one way, I could see my house and car and everything like I had always known it, and, if I looked another way, I saw farmland.

"Hell, I'll be honest. I thought maybe I was having some kind of flashback. Like I'd be the guy who dropped acid once and had flashbacks about rural America."

The double vision came and went throughout the rest of the day. That night, he dreamed he was at the Belle Meade Mansion and there was a huge party. He was dancing with three or four different young women who were all vying for his attention, all decked out in enormous ballgowns supported by layers of petticoats.

"It wasn't a dream," he said. "I woke up and I just knew it wasn't just a dream. It was so vivid, like when you dream about your kid being born, or the moment your wife tells you she wants a divorce. You dream about it like it happened. Only, obviously, it hadn't happened to me.

"In the morning, I called the police to find out what was going on. They told me that they'd turned the bones over to the state after determining that they were over 150 years old.

"'Probably that Harding kid,' the officer on the phone said, and when he said the name, it was like—I don't know—it was like my whole body just ached; like some part of me recognized that name.

"I called my ex-wife. I didn't know what else to do. I told her I thought I was possessed. She took it better than I thought she might. She did a bunch of research on drowned Harding kids.

"'George,' she said, 'His name was George.' I just busted out crying. Only it wasn't me. God, this is weird. But you see what I'm saying. I couldn't have cared less. But the kid in me did.

"And then, then I said, 'Ma'am, I would like to see my sister, if you can find her.' Only, obviously, I know where my sister is. But my ex, she was always much better about this weird stuff life throws you than I am. She says, 'Okay.'

"So she starts doing research, trying to track down this kid's sister. Meanwhile, now he's in my head. And he's freaked out. I mean, if I could keep the new stuff to a size he could manage, he was fascinated. He loved indoor lighting and television kind of blew his mind.

"But when I went to the grocery store I got stuck in the meat department, because he got all freaked out and afraid. I had to call my ex to come get me.

"I told her that if this kept up I was going to have to move back in with her, just so she could mother this kid, too. She even found that funny, which was nice.

"I know you didn't come to hear about my problems with my ex, but that was the moment when we became friends again. Hundred percent improved things for my kid. Weird as it was, I'm grateful to George for that.

"Anyway, so she found his sister. I mean, yeah, she found her buried over in Mt. Olivet. But more than that, his sister, Elizabeth Harding, was sent to stay with the other side of the family, out in Donelson, after George died.

"And now she haunts Two Rivers."

"Really?" I said. "Two ghosts in the same family?"

"You know that's how those two families are, right?"

"What two families?"

"The Hardings and the Donelsons. Being a ghost runs in both families. You see a ghost in Nashville you don't know, you just holler 'Harding' or 'Donelson' and chances are pretty good they'll turn around.

"So really, if it were any other family, yeah, I guess it'd be strange, but they're Hardings, so of course they're ghosts."

Now, I have to tell you, when *I* say this kind of stuff to other people, I don't think it sounds strange. I figure that if we're talking about ghosts, you're kind of prepared for any weirdness that might come up. But sitting there listening to Sharp talk about ghostliness running in old Nashville families? I admit, I had half a mind that he was crazy.

He continued, "So we arranged for a tour of Two Rivers mansion, claimed we were considering getting married there, and my ex took the lady who was showing us around off into a back room under some pretense and

George and I stood at the bottom of the stairs.

"'Is this where Liza lives?' he asked, and I said, 'Well, kind of. She's dead.' And he just started crying so hard I had snot all running down my face. 'What kind of terrible place is this?' he wailed. 'Everything looks different. Everyone I love is dead.' And I said, 'You know you're dead, too, right?' And I don't know if he just hadn't quite thought about it or what, but that thought seemed to calm him down. 'Why don't you go see if you can't find Liza?' I said, and he nodded and sniffled a little bit, and then there was this incredible pressure on my face, and I thought I might throw up. I opened my mouth and I pushed out my tongue, and it was like he just poured out of me.

"And then, he was gone."

"Just like that?"

"Just like that. But hey, his body's in his grave now and now I hear stories about a young man who haunts Two Rivers. So maybe he's okay?

"I hope he's okay, anyway. I never heard from him again."

October 14ᵗʰ

THE NASHVILLE TUNNELS

Every once in a while, someone will claim there are tunnels under downtown Nashville, linking the old buildings and running out to the river. What's strange is that is this obviously true. There are newer tunnels such as the storm water system under Second Avenue, or the tunnel that connects Legislative Plaza with the Capitol. And there are older tunnels through which heat and electric have been run. Shoot, Timothy Demonbreun and Elizabeth Bennett lived in a cave! Is a cave with two entrances not a tunnel?

So why, when you ask most folks if there are tunnels under downtown Nashville, do they say no?

This is the answer I heard from a man I'll call Elias. Elias isn't from Nashville. He'd flown in specifically to retrieve Rabbi Heiman's remains, if there were any. A friend of a friend got me a meeting with him over breakfast before he left again, never to return.

Here is what he told me, parts of which, obviously, had been told to him.

There is a series of tunnels running under downtown. Not utility tunnels, but honest-to-God secret passages, designed to allow people to sneak out of buildings unseen and down to the river.

Most of these tunnels were put in places shortly after the Civil War. Regardless of where their sympathies lay, the occupation was very difficult for the citizens of Nashville. Fields had been destroyed. Almost all of the trees had been cut or burned down. The streets were thick with soldiers and the attendant illicit businesses that sprang up to serve them. And then, after Lincoln's assassination, there was a very real fear that the Federal government would come into the South and annihilate it in retaliation.

People wanted protected escape routes. And so the tunnels were put in.

After the destruction of the city ceased to feel like an immediate threat, the tunnels started to serve other purposes. They became a way for white men to slip in and out of Black Bottom, unseen by disapproving neighbors; for liquor and prostitutes to make their way into "good" establishments; and by the early 1900s there were rumors of something else, that the tunnels had become a safe place for the worst kinds of men.

People disappeared in the tunnels. They went in and they never came out.

This was kept secret, as much as possible, by the town fathers because no one wanted the police to look into what else was going on in the tunnels.

But it was impossible to cover up the disappearance of Portia Rutledge, a lovely girl from a prominent family. She had been with her sister and her sister's husband, exploring the tunnels that ran from the brand-new Hume-Fogg school toward the river. Her sister and brother-in-law had turned a corner just moments before—mere seconds—and she was gone. She never rounded that corner.

They searched the tunnels as far as they could, but by 1920 it was a maze beneath the city streets. They came up for help and a search party was organized. For three days they searched, but there was no sign of her.

Weeks later, two street kids were in the tunnels, trying to escape the heat and the truant officer, when they heard faint sobbing. They followed the noise and, eventually, found Portia Rutledge's body, maybe a hundred yards from one of the Hume-Fogg tunnel entrances.

Elias said there wasn't a mark on her body.

This is where the story gets very strange. Portia Rutledge's body had been found within easy distance of a tunnel entrance, and yet no one would go in and retrieve it. Stranger still, the papers were still reporting her missing. People were speculating that she'd fallen in love with someone her family disapproved of and that she was probably living in Bowling Green, laughing at everyone still looking for her.

One of the families in Rabbi Heiman's congregation owned a dry-goods store downtown. And they had begun to hear a woman sobbing in the basement of their store. They mentioned this to Rabbi Heiman, who thought it was strange, but he assured them that the sobbing woman was probably just a prostitute living in the tunnels. He advised them to leave some bread on the other side of their tunnel entrance—just a little something to make her life easier.

Shortly after that, the owner of the store overheard the street kids talking, not only about the crying in the tunnels, but also the body their friends had discovered, and the store owner became very concerned. By the description the kids gave, he was certain it was Portia Rutledge. He was also becoming more certain that the sobbing in the tunnel was connected to her body being left in the tunnel. The shop owner went to see the rabbi and told him his suspicions and what he overheard the kids saying.

"Her body has been found," Rabbi Heiman said, "and yet no one has moved it?"

"I know this is not our concern," the shopowner said. "Maybe this is some kind of family tradition?"

But they both knew that was not true.

Rabbi Heiman mulled this over for days. He felt compelled to try to do something. He also knew that he might be placing his family and congregation in a great deal of danger if he in any way made it seem as if they could be blamed for her disappearance. Even connecting himself to her recovery might be enough to cast suspicion for her death.

"I should go look," Rabbi Heiman said to the shop owner.

"No, no," the shop owner said. "Let someone in the Chevra Kadisha go."

"No. If there is trouble with her people, I will be the most likely to get out of it," said the rabbi.

He decided to go into the tunnels through the basement of the dry-goods store and make his way up, unseen, to Hume-Fogg. He never made it that far, and he came out of the tunnel deeply shaken. The owner of the dry-goods store helped him sit on a crate. The owner's son brought him some water.

"Just a few blocks up," he motioned with his hand, before wiping his brow. "I started to hear footsteps, heavy footsteps, in front of me. I dimmed my lantern and ducked into a side tunnel. I could hear the footsteps getting closer and closer. Finally they were so loud I would have sworn there was a man not three feet from me. But I could see, even by dim light, that the tunnel was empty.

"I heard a voice, though. A man's voice. He said 'This ain't no place for a man of God, Reverend. Down here's all the stuff He don't see.'"

"And the girl?"

"I didn't find her. I will have to try again."

"Let her own people worry about her," the store owner said.

"But now I know," the rabbi said. "If I find her, I can leave a note for her family—tell them where to look."

The rabbi went down in the tunnels again the next day. He had been gone maybe an hour when the shop owner and his son heard distant screams.

"Rabbi?" the shopowner yelled into the tunnel entrance. "Rabbi!"

The two grabbed a lantern and started down into the tunnel. Far, far ahead of them, they saw a dim, shaking

146

light rushing toward them.

The rabbi was yelling, "Run! Go back! Go back!" They began to back up slowly, afraid to leave the tunnel without him. They were maybe five feet from the door to their basement. Their lantern cast a pool of light maybe ten feet beyond what came from the basement. And the man and his son both saw the rabbi, for a second, at the far edge of the darkness. "Go back," he said again.

And then he fell, or maybe his feet were yanked out from under him, and he hit the ground hard. The man scrambled forward to try to grab the rabbi, but the rabbi screamed, "No," and the man's son dragged the man back into the basement. The son slammed the door.

The man and his son tried later that day to search the tunnels for any sign of the rabbi. There was none. In the distance they thought they sometimes heard heavy footsteps, though.

Later, after the story got out that the rabbi had returned to St. Louis (a place the rabbi had never actually even visited), the man and his son blocked the tunnel at least a hundred feet beyond their door. Shortly after this, one of the other downtown business owners came to pay them a visit.

"You need to unblock the tunnel," he said. "You can do what you want in your own store, but those tunnels remain open. Do you understand? We have a deal that the tunnels remain open."

"Who has a deal?" the shopowner's son asked.

The businessman looked angry and frightened. "It's not any of your business."

Elias told me that other things had happened, things that made the shopowner's family very, very afraid, not of the thing in the tunnels, but of the other businessmen downtown. The rabbi's home burned down, for instance, and the rabbi's widow and his children barely escaped with their lives. They were sent to St. Louis, where it was thought they'd be safer.

The shopowner and his son began to put a little cash aside. Not even enough to be noticed—they didn't want to raise any suspicions at the bank or among the other businessmen, didn't want anyone gossiping about how strange it was that their profits were down, even as their foot traffic remained steady.

They set aside just enough so that whenever a hole was dug for a new building, they could pay a person to search whatever tunnels were discovered for the rabbi's remains.

Elias had been hired by the shopowner's grandson, himself now an old man, to get into the tunnels opened up while they were excavating the new convention center.

"And did you find him?" I asked.

"I did," he said quietly. "He was about a hundred yards from one of the Hume-Fogg entrances, just dust and bones and a few scraps of clothing. I was able to identify him by his cufflinks. Nearby was a woman's skeleton."

"Weird," I said. "Do you think he found her?"

"No, I think his body had been placed near hers after he was killed."

"My God. Did you recover her body too?"

"No," Elias said, quietly. "That was not my job."

"And what about that thing, that man? Do you think he's still down there?"

Elias stared at the people passing by us for a long, long time.

"I know he is," he said. "Let me ask you: do you think it's possible that he is worse now than he was? That killing a man of God could make him worse? Or do you think it's always been that bad down there? How could a city have sat

148

on top of that for a hundred years?"

"You said they mentioned something about a deal."

"Who would depend on a deal made with the likes of him?"

October 15th

THE WIDOW LEDBETTER

Most everyone can tell you that Jesse James was killed by Robert Ford. What most people cannot tell you is how Frank James managed to live until he was seventy-two. Was he not also an outlaw? Did people not die at his hand? How is it that Jesse died and Frank lived?

It seems luck. Or maybe Jesse was less likable than Frank.

If you ask around Fort Campbell, though, you hear a strange story:

Frank James lived to be an old man because any man who sleeps with the Widow Ledbetter is promised a death from natural causes at an old age.

This is trickier now than it was in Frank James's day because the Widow Ledbetter has long been deceased. But it still can be done.

Maybe it's best to start with Frank, who arrived in what is now Bordeaux with his wife, Anna, in July of 1876, sick with malaria and hunted by the authorities. He was calling himself Ben Woodson. Anna had changed her name to Fannie Woodson. They arrived at the home of Ben Drake, who lived along Hyde's Ferry Pike, and Drake recognized that Woodson was dying. He also suspected, looking at Mrs. Woodson's jewelry, that they were quite wealthy. He insisted they stay until Woodson was better. One night, after Fannie had gone to bed, Drake and Woodson were sitting at the table by the fire playing cards.

"Friend," said Drake, "You're not well. In fact, you may be dying."

Woodson sat silently for a long time, and then said, "May be."

Drake proceeded cautiously. "I have not asked you much about yourself."

"And I have appreciated that."

"As I have appreciated you not asking me much about myself. But tonight, I am going to tell you one thing about my family. The women in our family have a... shall we say... a gift."

"And what might that be?"

"Sir, I'm afraid there is no delicate way to put this."

Woodson laughed and shook his head, "Then it is good that I am not a delicate man."

"The women in my family can make men well."

"That's hardly unusual. My mother kept seven plants in her garden that could, in one combination, heal a man, and in another, kill him."

"Well, yes, that is part of the skill my sister has."

"And the other part?"

"She can give a man old age. Any man that... sleeps... by her side... will live to be an old man and will die of natural causes. No harm can come to him, except at her hand. And I can promise you that my sister has no more interest in harming anyone than ... well, I can guarantee that she is not a violent person. And she can cure you."

"For a price, I assume."

"Yes. Two-hundred and fifty dollars."

They had not seen Fannie come back in the room.

"Please, Ben," she said. "Please, let's at least try." It may sound, to our ears, hard to believe. But imagine Fannie's situation. She's on the run and in a place where she has no friends. Her only close family is her crazy brother-in-law, who was in hiding somewhere nearby. If Frank died, she would be on her own, hundreds of miles from anyone

152

who knew her and might take care of her, and she knew there was a baby on the way.

She herself, in fact, handed the money to the Widow Ledbetter, who, in turn, took Woodson's hand and led him to her room. I suppose it goes without saying what happened in that room. The important thing is that Woodson recovered, and, as promised, lived to be an old man.

And that might have been the end of it, except that Anna Ralston James lived until 1944 (make of that what you will) and she mentioned to a friend, whose son was going to fight in the Spanish-American War, that there was a woman near Whites Creek who could guarantee his safety. The son, the story goes, found the Widow Ledbetter and survived the war. That was, it is said, how it became an Army legend—fuck the Widow, live forever.

Okay, not forever, but you'd grow old. And that's almost the same as forever to a man who's being shot at.

I'm not sure how they learned how to make the deal with her after her death. But I have heard that during the Vietnam war, if a soldier said he was "going down 41," it was understood that he was going to Nashville to summon the Widow, and that soldiers stationed at Fort Campbell have been, from time to time, forbidden from getting off at the Old Hickory Boulevard exit. If they want to come to Nashville, they must go straight into the city—no hanging out on the outskirts of town.

Now that no one is sure where she's buried, this is how it's done. You must acquire a jar of water from Whites Creek, preferably from between Clarksville Pike and Hydes Ferry. You must also procure a heaping handful of dirt from the creek side. You need three white candles, flowers if you're feeling romantic and, of course, two hundred and fifty dollars.

Find yourself a room with a bed. Most folks now use the Super 8 out where I-24 crosses Old Hickory Boulevard, but you can still use one of the old motor lodges along

Clarksville Pike, if they have room.

Take a shower. Turn off all the lights. Light your three candles. Open up your jar and place the money in the creek water. Smear the dirt on your hands. As you do this, look into the mirror in the room, and repeat, *"Harriet Ledbetter, grant me long life. And just for this evening, I'll make you my wife."* over and over until she appears in the reflection of the mirror. Do not look directly at her until she touches you. And do not let her go until she lets go of you.

She will vanish at dawn and then you must take everything—the water, the dirt, the candle stubs, the money, flowers if you brought them for her—and dump it in Whites Creek as soon as you can. Toss it over your shoulder and leave without looking back.

I know, you're thinking, it's so easy. And if it works, why don't more folks do it? Why don't folks tell everyone?

I met a man who attributed his having lived through Vietnam to Harriet Ledbetter. He agreed to have French toast with me at the Hermitage Cafe, and I sat across from him and asked him that very thing.

He said the first thing that stops you is embarrassment. You don't want folks to think you're crazy. You don't want the folks who don't think you're crazy to think you're a bad Christian, summoning spirits, which the Bible expressly forbids.

The second thing is that it's not good, that night. Her skin feels and smells like cold, wet earth. Her breath smells like a cup full of night crawlers. And she looks at you like she knows some terrible secret you'll have to die to find out. And yet, when she touches a man, he responds.

And then, he explains, running a big, square hand through his shaggy gray hair, it ruins you after that. You cannot sleep alone, because if you do, you wake to find a corpse-cold leg thrown over yours, a dead hand resting knowingly on your chest. She is there when no other person is. And so you must work to always keep your bed filled.

"The guy I learned about her from?" the vet says, rolling the paper napkin between his fingers. "His wife died from breast cancer last year. He's only 62. His doctor says he's got another twenty years, maybe more. He don't want another woman. But what can he do? Any living woman is better than what's waiting for him otherwise."

October 16th

THE SYLVAN HEIGHTS SOLDIER

Sylvan Park has properly gentrified, and West End has had a fancy streak for as long as anyone can remember. But Sylvan Heights, wedged between the two of them, lying along the railroad tracks, is still waiting for its neighbors' good fortune to spread through it.

So a person cannot be blamed for not noticing at first that the neighborhood is haunted by Union soldiers.

After all, it's easy enough to assume, when you catch a figure skulking along the railroad tracks, that it's one of the hobos who lives in the camp on the other side of 440. And if you should be sitting in your living room and you hear the storm door open, see the doorknob shake as if someone is trying a locked door, and you bound across the room to see if it is your loved one home from work, and you throw open the door and find no one there, might not it have been just the wind?

It's harder to explain the mornings when you are out walking your dog down Park Circle, when you cross Acklen Park and you look down toward the curve and you see a man standing there, a plain wool blanket over his shoulders like a cape, and a strange hat. In the early dawn light you cannot make out much more than that—just a man in a blanket. You keep walking, and when you get to the next block, you look down Wrenwood toward the train overpass and you see a man—surely not that same man—hunched down in the middle of the intersection, watching you.

You should probably be afraid, but you have a big dog and a cell phone and you've spent most of your time in the city convincing yourself that those are all the tools a girl needs to ward off danger.

So you stand there, in your overalls and your winter coat, your pajamas still on under it all. Your breath making an icy cloud in the cold morning. If he has a breath, he's been holding it a long time.

Suddenly, right behind you, you hear "Ma'am?" and you turn toward the clipped Yankee accent.

There's no one there.

And when you turn back around, there's no one there either.

October 17th

THE LAST UNHAUNTED SPOT

Most people don't notice ghosts for the same reason you don't notice your own breathing. Air slips in and out of our bodies without us having to think too much about it. Our souls slip in and out of our bodies without us having to think too much about it. All the noise and motions ghosts make, going about their business, once we're grown, usually fades into the background, forgotten along with the rest of our imaginary friends.

We don't notice not because there's no such thing as ghosts, but because, in a sense, there is nothing *but* ghosts.

Except, weirdly enough, for one spot in the grass in front of Grace Baptist Church, where Brick Church Pike crosses Old Hickory Boulevard. The geography seems normal enough, but something about that place left it empty from the dead.

This is where that strange little gal from Goodlettsville would come on the nights when she couldn't sleep for all the racket. She would drive down, park in the parking lot, and lie down in the empty spot in the grass. Usually she would wake with the dawn, but the church secretary had also gotten used to shaking her awake and sending her on home.

After she died, the secretary would still see her lying there in the grass some mornings. Sometimes the secretary would walk toward her, but that gal would always fade from view before the secretary could get close to her.

Lots of folks saw her there, before and after her death, which led to a story about how she had been in an accident at that intersection and thrown from her car, where she landed in that spot and died, and that's why she haunts that place.

That's not the truth of how she died, but it almost doesn't matter.

Now there is no spot in Nashville that is not haunted.

October 18th

SULPHUR CREEK ROAD

Sulphur Creek Road doesn't appear on old maps, though there's a church along it that has had a congregation for a hundred and fifty years. It stretches between Old Hickory Boulevard and Eatons Creek Road, winding through that infamous northwest Davidson County terrain. Sharp hills, a tight hollow, turns that run you straight into trouble before you see it coming. A hundred years ago, it ran between land the Simpkinses owned and land the Hazlewoods owned.

They never used it.

A hundred and fifty years ago, it was common to smell the sour bite of mash in the still out there, which meant armed men with something to hide.

Two hundred years ago, it was difficult for white men to travel into this area, one of the last places the previous inhabitants were routed out of, those who did not disappear.

A long time ago, rumor started to spread that a person didn't have to go very far north to find freedom, that there was, for those brave enough to make a break for it, a place just outside of town, not quite to Ashland City, where, if you could get there, they couldn't get you back.

It only took two guns, they said, to defend it, the strategic advantage was so great. One at the north end of the hollow, up in the hill, and the other at the south end. Like early snipers, they could pick off a group of men on horseback before the riders even knew what direction the gunfire came from.

They say, even now, if you drive Sulphur Creek Road after dark, with your windows down and your radio off, you'll often catch a muzzle flash and hear the shot fired right at you, even if the folks who guard this place can no longer hurt you.

Even now, especially after dark, this is not a place strangers are welcome.

October 19ᵗʰ

SOMETHING NOT UNDER WATER

Sal and Evan were very fortunate. They had three feet of water in their house. They had to gut the kitchen and pull out all the drywall and carpeting. Everything that the water touched had to be gotten rid of or cleaned. Sal spent two hours one day cleaning their old tub. Spraying cleaner and wiping and spraying and wiping until she had a bag full of dirty paper towels, a bruised knee, and a clean place to shower. They lost so much, but not everything.

At first, the worst thing was the smell. It was everywhere in the house and in the neighborhood, a mixture of outhouse and stale fish tank. After a while, they weren't even sure if it was a real smell anymore or just the ghost of the smell taken up residence in their noses.

But then, for Sal, the worst thing was the dream. Long after it was over, she dreamed about the flood. Dreamed of floating in brown water, waiting for Evan to save her; dreamed that Evan was dead. Some days she would dream that she was standing on West End, in front of Vanderbilt, and she would see Evan coming up the hill from downtown and she would run to him and he would hug her to him and when he leaned in to kiss her, dirty water would pour out of his mouth into hers.

One time she woke from this dream and felt that her face was wet. She was already screaming before she realized she had just been crying.

Months passed. One day, Sal was on her knees in the bathroom, once again scrubbing the tub. And there, right at the drain but not yet slipped in it, was a small clump of blond hairs.

Neither Sal nor Evan was blond.

She went into the living room, where Evan was

163

watching baseball. She sat down next to him on the couch and handed him the hair.

"I just wanted something not under water," he said.

"A shower is water." It was not up for argument.

She walked out the front door, up the driveway, and into the road. She lay down.

And waited to die.

At first, no one noticed. Not even Evan. I think he thought she had gone to get the mail. After all, surely, if she was leaving him she would have taken her purse.

All afternoon, she lay there, her cheek hot against the asphalt, her outstretched hand collecting ants. Eventually some neighbor kids saw her and ran in to tell their moms. One of those mothers called Evan, who hurried out.

"Are you okay?" he asked, but she said nothing. "Come on," he said, "You're making a scene." But really, once your whole neighborhood has been underwater, what's one distraught woman in the road? "Fine. Fuck you, too." He stormed off and stood on the porch.

After a long time, a police officer showed up. Maybe we should have thought there was something weird right then. No one remembered seeing a police cruiser. And his hat was a little too "milkman," but the badge looked real enough.

He walked over to Sal. "Ma'am?" he asked, his voice more gentle than people expected. He was a bear of a man, tall and gray-haired. When he saw that she could not answer him, he sat down next to her. He crossed his legs, shifted his gun belt and reached down and took her hand.

He sat with her a long time, quietly whispering to her. Eventually, huge tears began to roll down her cheeks. She blinked in the afternoon sun and he helped her sit up.

"Damn Nashville drivers," she sniffed, finally

breaking a smile, "can't even run a gal over right."

He laughed too, and helped her to her feet. Only after she was safely on the porch and drinking the sweet tea that Evan brought her did the officer finally leave.

Shortly after that, a police car pulled up. "Did you guys see a woman in the road?"

"An officer already dealt with that," Evan said.

"There's no officer out this way but me," the cop said.

"Ask anyone," Evan said. "We all saw him."

"What did he say to you? What did you talk about?" the police officer asked Sal.

"We talked about how much he missed this place," she said, mostly to herself, "and how he would give anything, anything to have even the worst of it back."

October 20th

THE HAUNTING OF EASTLAND AND PORTER

There were two young men who went to the same church over on the east side of the river. As children, they were inseparable. Tom got married to his high school sweetheart and Danny, though not married when he died, was a well-known flirt who spent most of his time in the church choir making time with the women who surrounded him.

There had been rumors of trouble in Tom's life, and it was widely known in the church that he and his family had weekly meetings with the pastor, and it was widely accepted that he had been encouraged to marry so young as a way of setting aside his wild youth and aligning himself with God's will.

The young men were killed in a traffic accident at the corner of Eastland and Porter. Tom still had his motorcycle, and Danny needed a ride someplace after church. Now there is a three-way stop at that corner, but it used to be that only the person coming west on Eastland had to stop, and that person was at a distinct disadvantage when trying to see if anyone was coming toward him around the curve. You just had to go and hope no one was coming too quickly.

Tom was the oncoming traffic that day. He skidded up Porter, his motorcycle still between his legs. He died instantly. Danny was thrown clear and he died a few days later.

Since then, the spot has become a magnet for paranormal groups looking to investigate active hauntings. When Davidson County Paranormal League had their Halloween special on WKRN, this corner was one of their features, and flame wars erupted on local websites about whether the footage was faked.

The footage that had the whole city talking was of

two distinctly male voices. One calls out "Tom? Hey, Tom!" and, after a few minutes, the other calls out, "Danny? Are you really here?" And then there's a whoop and a scream and sobs.

The Davidson County Paranormal League explained that they considered this a residual haunting—that there weren't actually spirits still here, but that this was a moment in these men's lives so profound that the right conditions could cause it to replay, over and over.

In a psychology class up at Austin Peay, this clip was the centerpiece of a discussion of the group dynamics involved with believing in what the professor termed "this paranormal nonsense."

And so he played the clip for the class. And a woman in middle of the second row started to sob.

"Oh my gosh," she said, wiping her eyes, "I'm so sorry. That just hit me right in the heart. I know that noise."

"Are you saying that you have witnessed a ghost?" the professor was suddenly worried the lecture was about to go way off track.

"No, no," she said. "When my husband got back from Iraq, that's the noise he made when he saw me again for the first time."

It had not occurred to the professor that the noises at the end of the clip were noises of joy, of loved ones being reunited. But later, as he sat at his desk, playing the video over and over, he wondered how he had missed it.

When he got home, he told his husband about it. His husband, who grew up here, was perplexed for a long time.

"It's not obvious to you that the story is about two lovers?"

"No," the professor said. "My students got it, though. Some of them were uncomfortable with it, but it was clear to them from the noise."

"Well," said the husband, "that's something. In my day, it would have been clear to us from the young marriage, since she wasn't pregnant. Times change."

October 21st

THE DEMOSS HOLLOW HOUSE

There is a house in Demoss Hollow, just off River Road west of town, that is tucked so far back away that you can't see it from the road. It has the twin chimneys and the low slung porch that say that it was built a while ago. It has, at least, been there as long as anyone can remember.

It also has, for the most part, been empty.

"It wasn't the kind of place that seemed bad right away," one of the neighbors told me. "It was on my uncle's neighbor's land, and we used to go there all the time, stay there when we were hunting, hang out there when we should have been at school. It was up the hill a little way, so you could see out over everything. Beautiful view.

"So, we're sitting on the porch one day and we hear this voice, a gal's voice, and she says, plain as day, 'John, I will kill you.'"

"Were any of you named John?" I asked.

"Now, don't take this wrong, but I wished there was. Then at least we would have known it was one of our girlfriends or something. But no, none of us was John."

They looked around to see if they could find anyone, but they never did.

"Do you know Bub Dozier?" the neighbor man asked me.

"No," I admitted.

"His family goes way back here. Anyway, he married a gal from White Bluff and brought her back there until he could get them a house built up by his folks. And she hated that place. Said you'd be just about to sleep in the bedroom and you could hear someone in the kitchen, sounded like they were doing dishes.

"And one night, she was woke up by all the noise in the kitchen and she gets up and sets off down the hall and she swears there's no one in the kitchen, but the water glass that was in the sink is on a towel upside down, drying."

"Well, it'd be nice to have a ghost to do your dishes, I think," I said.

"You're kind of an idiot, aren't you? You think it's fun not knowing in your own house that you can put something down and come back to find it in the same place? That ain't fun. It's horrible."

"I'm sorry," I said. We sat in silence for a while.

"Aw, hell, it's just that if you haven't seen it, you don't know. And if you have seen it, you can't get no comfort because everyone thinks you're nuts."

"You've seen it?"

"Bub got real sick one fall," he said. "He wasn't going to go to the doctor, of course, but his wife called me up and begged me to make him." He drummed his finger into the table to punctuate his point. "She begged me." He took a long drink of coffee. "Doctor said that he'd been poisoned. Called the police over it, too. Well, of course, they thought his wife had done it. Hell, *I* thought his wife had done it.

"So they set bail, but no one would get her out. I said I'd stay with Bub.

"And I start to notice weird things. Like I'd go into the bathroom and the closet door would be open, even though I'd know neither of us had been in there. Hell, I wasn't doing their goddamn laundry, and Bub wasn't on his feet. Or you'd find coffee cups right by the coffeemaker in the morning, all by themselves.

"And that..." he looked over his shoulder, like he was trying to decide whether to say something. "... I think that's how she did it. A couple of times there was something in the bottom of the cup, some white stuff, looked like a fine dusting of sugar. You might not have even noticed it, if you hadn't realized already that the cups were strange. But I pick one up and I'm looking in it and I see that powdery stuff on the bottom.

"Now, I knew it wasn't me. It couldn't have been Bub, and his wife was sitting in jail. So, finally, I yell, 'Who the hell are you?' and…"

"Holy shit."

"I don't hear nothing. So, I shout, 'Are you the one looking to kill John?' and I swear, right as I said 'John,' that coffee cup just tore up out of my hands and slammed against the ceiling and broke into pieces.

"'Bub,' I said, 'There's something wrong with this place. We got to get you out of here and burn it to the ground.' So, I get under him and I'm lifting him up, and I hear this low voice, like a whisper, but a little louder, a man's voice. 'Wait.'

"'What'd you say, Bub?' But he didn't say nothing. I stand real still, with Bub kind of draped over my shoulder, and I whisper back, 'What?' and I swear, I hear, 'Don't burn it. Don't let her loose.'"

"What did you think that meant?"

"Hell if I know. You're supposed to be the one who can make sense of this stuff." Again, it was quiet for a long time.

"That house is still there," he finally said. "But we don't let nobody live in it."

173

October 22ⁿᵈ

Years ago a couple, the Andersons, moved to a little house on Ordway. Their neighbor was a little old man named Tim Macon who lived alone now that his wife had died and his children had moved north. He was a perfectly delightful neighbor. He'd come over to help Mrs. Anderson dig bulbs. He could be counted on to watch the dog while they were on vacation. And when Mr. Anderson needed someone to stand under the hood of his old beater with him, Mr. Macon was knowledgeable and brought beer.

And one day, Mr. Macon died. He sat down to rest on the swing on his front porch and never woke back up. It was as mild a death as one might have. Which is, perhaps, why it didn't seem to slow him down.

When the new neighbors moved in, the wife came running over to the Andersons' one morning, almost in tears.

"I smelled bacon," she said, as she started to calm down. "I heard bacon frying in the kitchen. I thought it was my husband. But he was still in bed with me. We went into the kitchen and…"

"There was bacon?" Mr. Anderson asked, half teasing.

"No, there was nothing, nothing but the smell of bacon frying in the pan."

They calmed her down, convinced her she was dreaming, and sent her home.

Three days later, she was back.

"Come now," she ordered. "Come now."

They ran next door and, plain as day, they could smell cigarette smoke. Not the stale smell that might work its way out of paint or carpet, but fresh cigarette smoke.

"We don't smoke," the neighbor husband said.

"Mr. Macon?" Mrs. Anderson asked. "Is that you? Now listen, you are scaring the pants off these poor people. Why don't you come and live with us? You know we don't mind."

I heard this story from the neighbor, which is why she remains nameless. She says that, after this, she never had any problems in the house—no ghostly bacon, no cigarette smoke.

But here's the weirdest thing. So, years go by and the property values on Ordway go up and the Andersons decide to sell their house and move out on Lickton Pike, in the country. The new people who bought the Anderson's house, after about six months, came over to the neighbors' and said, "You're not going to believe this..."

"Cooking bacon?"

"How'd you know?"

"That's our old homeowner."

"What should we do?"

"I don't know. I'd call the Andersons and ask them."

And you know what? The Andersons came back to their old house, told Tim Macon that he was frightening this set of homeowners and that Lickton Pike was lovely. He should come and stay with them out there.

And it worked.

October 23rd

THE CAT THAT SAID "MA MA"

The women who worked Dickerson heard the cat days before they saw it. The noise sounded almost like a human voice—words in the distance not quite made out. But the working girls had, if they had been on the street any length of time, learned to ignore voices not directed at them.

It was just safer that way.

But my God, can you imagine when the one of the noises they began to hear was "ma ma"? Women who had children they hadn't seen in weeks would gasp and shake. Girls who had come to miss their mothers so desperately would cry.

When the cat finally showed up and started to follow the women, for some it was a relief, when you could see the cat and see its open mouth and know the noise was coming from it, they thought it seemed cute and they called it "baby."

For others, seeing it only made it worse, made it seem more unnatural, and they called it "demon."

The police did not know about the cat, of course. So it's hard to know if the disappearances really started after the cat appeared. Women along Dickerson Pike have a habit of disappearing. Some go home. Some move on. And some just vanish.

The women contend that they are often preyed upon and that it's ignored. In the time the cat would follow them as they walked and waited for men in cars to stop, seventeen of them went missing in Nashville, six who worked Dickerson, meaning six who had heard the cat.

Every time a woman was arrested, she mentioned her missing friends.

If anything was being done about it, if they were even able to raise an alarm, they didn't know. (A file was started, a detective was assigned. But he knew those women, he thought, and thought they'd probably just found something else to do with their time.)

The women did what they could to keep each other safe—stood together, made sure every man who pulled over saw that someone else had seen his face. And yet, one by one, over the course of the next three months, four more women disappeared.

With tensions running high, you can hardly blame the woman who, when the cat showed up to follow her, grabbed it and tossed it into the street. It was hit by a car, but managed to limp off.

Later that evening, she bent over to peer in a car window and saw the man in the car had a cast on his right wrist. At first, she didn't think anything of it.

"Wanna date?" she asked.

"Ma ma?" He grinned so wickedly at her.

"Excuse me?"

"Ma'am?" He smiled, like he was going to play it off that she misheard him.

"It was that damn cat," she said later, "Or that damn cat was that dude. Either way, I didn't get in that fucking car, believe me."

Later, a different car, a different man, a different girl, still a right wrist in a cast.

"I'm looking for a place on Front Street."

"There's no Front Street, Mister."

"I've visited a doctor on Front Street before."

"In Nashville?"

"It's so easy to get lost when all the roads change

names."

"Shit, you're creepy. You go find Front Street on your own."

What happened next is not the kind of thing any person wants to admit. They killed the cat. They killed the cat, put it in a garbage bag and hid it in the basement of the Congress Inn, a motel they all were quite familiar with.

A week went by, and no man with a cast in any car, and no women went missing from Dickerson Pike. Another week, another, and then another.

Then one night they saw four police cars go by, lights flashing. The cars stopped at the Congress Inn and a body was pulled out of the basement. It was, of course, not the cat. It was, of course, a man with his right wrist in a cast, badly decomposed.

Even still, weeks went by and no women disappeared.

Because weeks went by and no one claimed that body. Until finally, it was cremated.

The women didn't know this, but they knew, soon enough, that almost-human voice, crying "Ma ma" in the dark. And they knew, soon enough, that one of them would disappear.

One of them, a woman they called Krissy, said, "We should have hid that body better, put it someplace where we could keep an eye on it but no one else could find it."

That was the problem, though, of course. Where could they put a body that would remain unfound? He knew. He knew where to put them where no one could find them. But they were not monsters.

"We have to put him someplace and then we have to keep folks away from there," Krissy said.

"And how are we going to do that? Who's going to stay there and keep folks away?"

And Krissy said, "I will."

The cat was captured again, eventually. And killed, again. And its body was brought, again, to the basement of the Congress Inn, along with bricks and mortar.

I have heard it both ways—that Krissy was dead by her own hand before they put her behind the wall, guaranteeing that she would not rest because of her unholy death and I heard that she helped brick herself up from the inside. But that's almost too much to think about.

I just know that when you go into the basement of the Congress Inn and you feel like the proportions are wrong, that the basement is smaller than it should be, that the voice you hear whispering in your ear, the tap on your shoulder that sends you scurrying back up stairs, they call that Krissy.

And I asked the woman who told this to me if she thought it was true. She looked away from me for a long time and then said, quietly, "I just hope that place never burns down."

October 24ᵗʰ

No one is sure if the thing on 18th Avenue North actually constitutes a ghost. But no one is sure what else to call it. Some say that you can almost see it on rainy or foggy days—a shape, like a person but not quite, around which the moisture bends as the shape moves down the street.

Kids say dirt will do the same, hit it and deflect, and it's not unusual to see kids walking from the corner where 18th and Clarksville Pike split going north toward Potter's Field kicking up dust in front of them, trying to get a glimpse of the thing before they step into it.

Because stepping into it is like stepping into old grief. It's the step you took, hands tight on your grandmother's casket, as you helped slide her into the back of the hearse. The first step you take after you hang up the phone from hearing, "I'm sorry but your son is dead." The moments you pray to forget and can't.

No one knows if it's a person or just a bad feeling that lingers between the Jewish cemetery and Potter's Field. But it sticks with you once you've felt it.

So people do what they can to avoid it.

This weird patch is not the most disturbing ghost on 18th Avenue North, though. That honor goes to a young boy who is often seen playing just inside the gates of the Jewish cemetery.

"I finally told them," the cop told me, "that if you see a white kid in the Jewish cemetery, do not even bother to call us about it. There haven't been white kids in that neighborhood in decades—I mean, like seventy years—and the gate is locked. No one is letting their seven-year-old climb the fence and play in the cemetery. That kid's not real. Do not call me."

I waited for him to settle down. He looked down at his plate of food and continued. "I mean, I sure as hell do not want to ever, ever see that kid."

"Who is he?"

"The Judge."

Soon enough, I was walking into the barbershop that sits kitty corner from the Jewish cemetery, and the three men in the place looked at the officer I was with like he had just violated all rules of social decorum.

"She's asking about the Judge."

"No," said one guy.

"No way," sad the second.

"I know," said the third.

"Will you tell me?" I asked.

"Hell no," said the first man.

The third settled into the barber's chair and rested his head against the back.

"My dad used to run this place and he would tell me about how when he was a kid, there used to be kids who worked in the mills over in Germantown. Small kids. Or how you'd go downtown and there'd be these kids on the corners selling newspapers or stealing apples out of the barrels that sat on the sidewalks. Some folks wanted those kids in school, thought they were a menace and needed to be off the streets. Other folks said that they couldn't run their businesses without those kids.

"Bad shit ... sorry, miss, bad stuff would happen to those kids sometimes. The Judge, my dad said, was beat to death by a man right downtown, in broad daylight. Worst part was that they just left that kid, like trash on the sidewalk. When his mother got off work, she came to look for him and found him in a heap, people just walking around him.

"He's buried right there." The third barber motioned across the street. "My father saw him once. He was sitting in this window and a white man pulled up in his car and got out and started coming toward the door. A few seconds later, a little boy just a few years younger than my father was then, appeared and seemed to be hurrying to catch up with the man.

"He had some business with my grandfather, that man. I don't know what it was. Times were different then, and you sometimes had to make some unsavory deals to keep your family safe. 'Sir, your son doesn't have to stand outside,' my grandfather said. And my father said that they all looked out the window and there was the small boy, just standing on the sidewalk, staring in.

"The white man went pale and started to shake. They tried to offer him a seat, but he rushed out, got in his car, and drove off. My father says that he looked right into the face of that boy. They weren't maybe three or four feet apart. You can see how close that sidewalk is. Just separated by glass. And my father says he didn't think anything strange of him. He just waved at the kid and the kid, for the first time, smiled and waved back, and then ... and I am not even joking ... he just faded from view.

"Now, I heard from some white folks, and you might try to find them if you can, that that kid followed the man who killed him everywhere, for the rest of his life. Everyone saw him, all over town.

"And when that man finally died? No cemetery would take him. When that kid died he was just trash. But by the time that man died, that kid was the victim of a monster. You know what I'm saying? People couldn't ignore what he did or just pretend like that's just what happened to kids. And they didn't want a child killer in their cemetery.

"So they put him in the field there. My wife will tell you he doesn't rest easy—that he's the bad spot. I worry about that kid, but she says the kid seems all right, not scared or sad, but where he wants to be."

"That's not what Granny Rose says," the cop said, and I realized I was in the middle of a longstanding family discussion. "She says that kid is just waiting there for bad men. That even now he can tell if you hurt little kids and he will torment you until you die. He just needs those bad guys to come close enough."

"Then why are you afraid of him?" the third barber asked.

"Dad, that stuff is scary. I don't care. It's weird and it creeps me out," the cop said. I thought for a second he might storm out and leave. But when he got to the door, he turned back around and he said, "And I don't want to stop him. If he does what Granny Rose says? Good. Most of the time, it's more than we can do."

October 25*th*
THE WOMAN IN THE HOUSE ON SIGLER STREET

Delia Patton was the last of her Pattons, the last of at least seven generations of Nashville Pattons stretching back before the War. Her mother had this theory that sometimes the old lines just petered out, which was the kind of thing that made sense on the surface, but not if you thought about it too hard.

After all, who were all these people from, if not old families?

Delia was a student at Lipscomb University. Even so, she spent most nights tangled so close to her roommate that she fell asleep to the gentle rush of her roommate's breath on her face.

She knew for her roommate this was just one impossible fling before she found a nice man and settled down and got married.

And she knew for herself, this made impossible the nice man and the marriage.

Once she knew that, she had this dream.

She dreamed she was in the house on Sigler Street. In real life she had never been in it, but she knew the stories; they were family stories. She was opening a closet and rummaging through the clothes. In the pocket of a light flowered housecoat was a silver skeleton key.

The key fit the lock on the hope chest in the front bedroom.

And the chest was opened.

There, on the top of some old quilts, was a note. The note said, "You could make me tell you I loved you a million times, but I never meant it. Not once. You might kill me, but I will kill all of you."

Delia woke with a start. Her heart was racing in her chest and her whole head was swimming. She had no reason to think what the note said was true. It was just a dream of an old family legend.

But she knew it was. Not how it was true, exactly, but she knew it was.

And that she couldn't shake.

Years later, she did get married. Times change. Still, when they decided to have children, she insisted her wife be the biological mother, just in case it was a blood curse.

October 26*th*

THE COVINGTON QUILT

It would be best if we didn't mistake Bettie Covington and Alice Pettis for friends. They had known each other their whole lives and they shared a common interest. Some say that Bettie was born into slavery on Alice's father's farm. I don't know if that's true. but I know their history went back before the War. I think, in their own ways, they were fond of each other, but no, not friends.

Even after Bettie got married, she would still spend at least one Saturday morning a month with Alice. They would start out in Alice's garden, both examining every plant and reminding each other what they'd been taught it was for, and then they would wander through the field, down to the stand of trees by the creek, doing the same.

Alice had learned three sure signs of impending death—a crow that catches your eye and lifts up his right foot (his left foot means bad news), a white blossom on a pink rose, and a dream of a saddled horse with no rider—which she taught to Bettie. And Bettie knew a sure way to make a person sicken and die without touching him—which she taught to Alice.

Here is one example of how they were not friends. The method Bettie taught Alice was to get a lock of hair from your victim, collect the water from your last night's chamber pot, and put both in a green bottle, which you then stop up and bury at the foot of a September elm. As the urine slowly dries up, so too does your victim's vitality.

It's a terrible way to go, but almost completely untraceable back to the person who's worked it.

When Alice discovered that Bettie was working it on the Davidsons, she beat her.

Alice thought she was saving Bettie from a worse fate.

Bettie knew Alice was damning the Davidson's housekeeper.

Still, even with her wrist still tender and her eye still purple and sore when she closed it, Bettie went back to the Pettis farm. And kept going back, until Alice and her husband moved to Nashville.

They moved back after the Davidsons died. (Their carriage overturned as they were headed to church. "See?" Alice asked Bettie. "The Lord didn't need your help in the matter." Bettie's face betrayed nothing, "Yes. Miss Alice.") Bettie sent her daughter, Josie, to work for the Pettises.

"But you don't even like them," her daughter complained, dropping her shoulders and sighing.

"Better the devil you know ..." her mother said.

Once Josie was working for the Pettises, many evenings after dinner were spent with Alice and Josie quilting. They worked through quilts for all the Pettis children, of whom there were many, and the Alice said "You should take these scraps and see what you can make of them."

This quilt is now, at least in certain circles, quite famous.

But it's not the quilt of Josie's that was most famous in her lifetime. The quilt she was most famous for in her own lifetime was the quilt that killed Alice Pettis.

And this is how she came to make it. She had just gotten into the kitchen one morning and was in the middle of stirring the coals and getting the oven going when she heard a terrible scream. She ran upstairs to find Alice doubled over in the hallway.

"Go get your mother," Alice said.

"Are you all right? Let me help you back to bed," Josie tried to put her arm around the woman, but Alice pushed her away.

"Now! Go get your mother now!"

And so Josie ran as fast as she could to her mother's home and the two of them came as quickly as they could hitch the mule to the wagon.

Bettie ran upstairs to Alice's side. Josie went to get a pitcher of water. When she got to the top of the stairs, she could hear her mother and Alice speaking.

"I can stop this," Alice said, "with Josie's help."

"And his," Bettie said. "Be honest. His help, too."

"Yes," Alice said, quietly.

"Then you can't have my Josie's help," Bettie said. "You can't ask her to do that."

Alice sat in her chair for a long time, her hand pressed against her mouth. Finally, she said, "Josie will do it," and she waited to see if Bettie was going to make her say any more than that out loud. When she saw that neither Covington was going to challenge her, she stood up and said, "I'm going to Franklin to get the things we'll need. I'll be back tomorrow, or the next day at the latest."

After she'd gone, Bettie took Josie into the kitchen where they could speak without being overheard.

"Miss Alice had a dream one of her children would die," Bettie said.

"Well, that's just a dream," Josie said, but her mother hushed her.

"No, Miss Alice can dream the future. If she sees it, it will happen. She's going to have you make a quilt. In the center, you should piece a seven-pointed star. I reckon she's only going to bring back black cloth, but still, you should piece it together just like you would any other quilt. When the time comes for quilting, someone will come to help you. Now, listen carefully. No matter what this person looks like, even if it looks like me, do not believe it. Look into a mirror to see its true form. Do not make this person angry, but do not agree to anything he or she says. Listen carefully. If he says 'May I have some water?' do not say 'Yes.' Say something like 'I can get some water from the kitchen.' Or if he says, 'Could you pass me that thread?' you say 'Which spool?' Like that. Do you understand? Don't agree with anything he says. Don't agree to do anything he says. He will seem very pleasant, I have no doubt. Do not be fooled."

"Yes, Mama," Josie said. She was trembling, but she didn't know why.

"And when you are done, run," Bettie said, tears starting to fill her eyes. "Do not come to me. Do not come to a soul who knows you. Change your name."

"Will I ever see you again?" Josie asked.

"I will find you after I am sure he's gone, but it may be a long while," Bettie said.

When Alice returned, she had yards of black cloth. Josie did as her mother had instructed and pieced together a seven-pointed star in the middle and then cut the rest of the fabric into squares and triangles and rectangles, which she rearranged back into a quilt top.

When she and Alice had finished getting the back, the batting and the top all onto the frame, there was a knock at the front door.

"Why don't you get that, Josie?" Alice said.

"Yes, Miss Alice," Josie made her way to the front door and opened it. A very tall, very slender blond woman with a large bustle that made her look almost like an ant stood before her. "Please come in," Josie said to the woman. "Miss Alice is in the parlor." As Josie turned to indicate the way, she caught a glimpse of the woman in the large mirror in the front hall.

In the mirror, he had black eyes and long, black hair, tied up in the same fashion as she had her blond hair in front

190

of Josie. In the mirror, his shoulders moved under the fabric of her dress like a cat stretching up from a nap.

Before she could stop herself, Josie was imagining herself under those skirts, his hot thighs in her hands. He caught her eye in the mirror and winked so long and slow Josie felt her knees give way beneath her. He licked his lips.

Josie turned away, embarrassed.

"So, you see me?" the blond woman asked.

"Ye—" Josie caught herself. "I see who you are, ma'am."

The woman purred to herself, just a little. "Well, best not get distracted. We have a long night ahead of us. Have you ever made a quilt before?"

"I know what I'm doing," Josie said, though, in truth, she wasn't sure.

"Hmm," the woman grinned. "It seems so."

And so they sat down, the three of them, and began to quilt. The blond woman told long stories about the strange things that happen near her home in Nashville. Alice made polite small talk. Josie said nothing.

They worked for hours, but Josie never got tired or hungry. And when the quilt was finally done, Josie remembered her mother's words, and stood up, "Excuse me," she said.

"Don't you want to stay and see what happens next?" the blond woman asked, and though Josie did, she just excused herself again and then ran off into the early dawn.

Years later, Alice's son, Samuel, was shot in a hunting accident. It looked as if he would surely die. He was brought back to the house and set in his childhood bedroom. His mother went to a chest, opened it, and pulled out the black quilt. She laid down in the bed with Samuel, who had his whole life ahead of him, and pulled the quilt over them. They both fell to sleep.

In the morning, he woke up. She did not.

That very same morning, a few miles away, Bettie Covington was just getting out of bed. She was startled, but not surprised to see Alice Pettis in the doorway.

"So, you got what you wanted," Bettie said.

"I am truly sorry," Alice said.

"Not as sorry as you will be, Alice," Bettie said, "when he catches up with you."

Alice was a bit taken aback. Their whole lives, Bettie had always called her "Miss Alice."

"Will you take the quilt?" Alice asked. "Bring it here and destroy it, if it can be? Hide it, if it can't?"

"Your troubles aren't my problem anymore," Bettie said. She shuffled through Alice into the kitchen. She rummaged around, grabbed a pinch of salt, and threw it at Alice. "Now leave me be."

For many years, the quilt stayed in the Pettis family, though it remained in a locked chest. Whenever anyone would take it out, a woman's voice could be heard, plain as day, "No, no," she would say, "No, no."

Rumor has it that the quilt spent some time in the basement of the Triune Methodist church before being donated to the Tennessee State Museum. The museum tried, once, to display it, but so many people asked about the docent in period clothing, standing by the quilt that the corporeal employees demanded it be put away.

October 27th

DUTCHMAN'S CURVE

There was a noise many folks mistook for the whistle at the prison and then an incredibly large explosion and then it was quiet. Just the sound of the wind rustling through the corn. You'd think that people would start screaming and crying out right away, but that's not so. You need a moment to wait for your brain to accept that what has happened has actually happened.

Even then, it doesn't seem quite real. And if you aren't in the middle of it, if you just hear about it, something so terrible, like two trains slamming into each other in the middle of a corn field, bodies and body parts tossed in with tattered luggage, it's even harder to say, "Yes, this terrible thing happened here."

The Monday after the flood, for instance, while people were still waiting to be rescued, while folks were just reentering homes to see how much they'd lost, while the police still blocked off roads, while the dead still remained uncounted, even while we were still shaken from the water that had just receded from our yard, we got in the car and went to look.

We smelled the putrid water. We walked to its edge and cried at the thought of the streets beneath it.

And we felt it, finally, in our bones—that this terrible thing had really happened, and that we had seen it.

So, I understand why so many Nashvillians—as many as 50,000 in a city that in 1918 had just over 100,000 residents—came out to see the aftermath of the great train wreck. How could you really know it unless you actually saw it? And how could you grieve it if you didn't know it?

These are the ghosts that upset people, though. Many times I've heard from people who have been walking down the Richland Creek Greenway or standing there at the site of the wreck, reading the signs or gazing up at the track, trying to imagine what it must have been like, and they will catch out of the corner of their eye, a great crowd of specters approaching.

"How could they come to gawk?" I'm asked.

But when we go there, looking for ghosts, hoping to hear the century-old echoes of the dying, are we not also gawking?

Are we somehow less ghoulish?

THE COUCHVILLE LIGHTS

Back then, they had a way of raising children as if the Devil was in them and your foremost job as a parent was to drive him out. Not every parent took this way, but it was considered best if you minded your own business if that's how your neighbor chose to raise his.

Even in that climate, folks were worried that John Higgins would kill his son, Pete. It was pretty common for folks to be sitting up at the Couches' grocery store and the subject of Pete would come up. Should someone go check on him? Should someone try to get in contact with his mother's people? Should the pastor talk with John about it?

If two or three days went by and no one had seen Pete, one of the Couch boys would be dispatched to make sure he was still alive. One time, the orneriest of the Couch boys had arrived out at the Higgins' farm to find John whaling on Pete with a belt while Pete was curled up on the ground. That Couch boy tried to get between them and John beat the shit out of him.

That resulted in some of the townsmen going out to the farm and having a little talk with John, but it didn't improve Pete's lot any.

There was some thought that once Pete got John's size, it would end. Pete would turn on him just once, drop the old man and that would settle it.

That turned out to not be the case. Pete never stood up to him. He would wake up, go through his day—doing his chores, sometimes running to town, come on home, make dinner for the both of them—and whatever his dad did to him, Pete just took it.

When he was fifteen, his dad did finally kill him. And even old John Higgins knew this was a bridge too far. Folks will overlook a lot—even pounding on someone else's kid—but they won't overlook a murder.

And so he waited until nightfall and carried Pete's body down to Stone's River, slit his throat, and dropped him in. It'd been a wet enough spring that the river was deep enough to carry that boy clear out of sight.

Old John figured that in the morning he would raise a fuss about the boy running off, and most everyone would figure Pete had finally got fed up, and that would be the end of it.

And so he came home, kicked his boots off and finally fell asleep. It's said that he dreamed of his dead wife, but I think folks just throw that detail in there to try to suggest there was something redeemable about him.

In the morning, John awoke to the sound of a pan clanking on the stove and, after a second, the smell of breakfast cooking. He opened his eyes, slowly rolled out of bed, and stumbled to the kitchen. There was Pete, same as always, fixing up some eggs and bacon.

John's first thought was, "Well, damn, I guess I didn't kill him." So, he sat at the table, like any other morning, and waited on breakfast. When the boy came close to drop the plate in front of him, John noted that he smelled wet, and when the father looked up at the son, John saw a red gash, like a grin, running from ear to ear under the boy's chin.

Now, I imagine John was terrified at first, but it became pretty quickly apparent that other than Pete being dead, circumstances didn't change much. Pete still fixed all the meals, still did all his chores and some of John's, and still wrangled the mule and the two pigs. Even the dog would still curl up at Pete's feet. The only difference was the Pete never talked and never slept. At night, even though it was getting warm, all he wanted to do was sit by the fire.

Pete'd make his way up to the store every once in a while and folks would stop to stare, but no one was quite sure what to do. They all knew he was dead. Shoot, the longer he was up walking around, the more apparent it became. His skin took on a translucent gray tone and sometimes he'd come in with a broken finger all hanging loose and crooked at the end of his hand. And, of course, there was the gash at his throat.

Finally, the orneriest Couch boy, himself nearing 18, had had enough.

"Y'all let that bastard kill him," he said in disgust, "and now you're going to let that be his afterlife?"

"Well, what are we supposed to do?" They asked. "It's not really our business."

"Maybe we really ought to get in touch with his mama's people," they said.

"Are you kidding me?!" Couch said. "My whole life... my whole life...and even still..." He shook his head and walked out of the store in disgust.

Late that night he made his way over to the Higgins place. He peered in a window and saw the bedroom door shut. Pete sat by the fire, staring at nothing. Couch knocked softly on the window. Pete slowly turned his head and looked. Couch lightly knocked again. Pete came to the door, unlocked it and stepped outside.

"Hey," Couch said, softly. "Are you all right? Pete, you know you're dead, right?"

And Pete nodded, his big eyes filling with tears.

"Then why are you still here?"

And Pete said, in a cracking voice that hadn't spoken in months, "I can't find my soul."

Couch didn't quite know what to make of it. "Excuse me?"

Pete just repeated, mournfully, "I can't find my soul."

Couch said, "Well, where did you last have it?"

And Pete said, "When I was five. I put it in a bottle and hid it so it'd be safe and my Dad couldn't break it."

Well, this Couch may have been the orneriest of the bunch, but even he could not hear this and not get a little choked up.

"Okay," Couch said, "Okay. Where did you hide it?"

"I remember putting it under the porch," Pete said. "But I got problems. My head only stays on if I stay upright. My fingers keep breaking. And I dug as much as I could, but..."

"Well, you're in a spot," Couch said. "But I'm going to help you. You just get your Dad good and drunk tomorrow night and while he's sleeping, I'll hunt for you."

And so, as planned, the next night John was passed out in the bedroom, and Pete, as best as he was able, was helping Couch pry up the floorboards on the porch so that Couch could dig beneath them. Finally, as it was getting on near three, Couch hit something hard in the dirt.

"Hey, Pete!" he yelled, without even thinking about it. "I got it."

Well, that was enough to wake John. He jumped up out of bed, grabbed his gun, and came rushing through the house, straight to the front door. He saw only that the porch was in ruins and someone he didn't immediately recognize was standing in front of him.

He fired twice.

Couch fell where he stood, the shovel dropping and, in a small miracle, shattering the glass jar half unearthed at his feet.

At the same moment, Pete fell to the ground, dead again.

A cool blue ball of light rose up out of the broken jar

and slowly drifted down toward the river. And then, they say, Couch's mouth fell open and a green ball of light rose up out of him and bobbed along behind the blue light.

They say John Higgins never even made it to trial, that he hung from the big oak in front of the grocery store before the judge got out that way.

And for years, people reported seeing those lights, two bobbing orbs, rising up out of the ground where the Higgins place used to stand and dancing all the way down to the river and beyond, finally, out of sight.

Years later, Couchville was given up to make room for Percy Priest Lake. Everything—the old grocery store, the post office, the Couch family home, even the old burnt-out ruins of the Higgins place—everything is underwater now.

And yet still those lights come up. You can see them coming up through the water, casting a soft glow on the skeletons of old buildings as they rise, and then they'll bob up out of the water and dance across the surface of the lake, headed up toward the Cumberland and points further.

October 29ᵗʰ

THE SUNDAY SCHOOL PUBLISHING BOARD OF THE NATIONAL BAPTIST CONVENTION, USA, INCORPORATED

Cities scar and bruise like people do. A wound opens and tissue builds around it when an interstate slices through a neighborhood. Folks will worry the loss of a beloved church like they worry the tender spot where a tooth has gone missing.

And then, in some cities, there are spots where the routine evil done there can make a place feel gangrenous. You turn your head from it. You catch your breath in your throat. You deliberately stop knowing what went on there. It was something that happened a long time ago. Something that doesn't matter anymore.

And you make your way past it like that city block is the shadow at the far end of a dark hallway. You will yourself to not look. You will yourself to not see. You close your eyes and dash past and feel like you have just avoided having to know something about how the world works that you can't explain.

Such was the case for the old hotel at the corner of Cedar and North Cherry. Patrons would complain about the loud cries and moans and wails. Other patrons would complain about the spectral men who stood outside their doors, engaged in casual discussion about selling people using words polite people now kept quiet.

In the 1920s, $300,000 was both a lot to pay for that building and not nearly enough. But part of the reason the building was even within reach of the Sunday School Publishing Board was that the hotel could never figure out a way to overcome the unique challenges of that spot.

The Sunday School Publishing Board, however, does have a way.

There are always two employees—one man and one woman—who have been specially trained and whose job it is to deal with the past still bleeding into the present.

Everyone else is reminded regularly to lift the two employees up in their prayers.

The job is difficult, because all who come are helped.

When it is as simple as squatting down low in the dark basement and holding out your hand to a scared child who wants nothing more than to be reunited with his mama, the job is merely heartbreaking. When the spirit is angry and trapped and disgusted that the only help for him comes from the likes of you, it takes a very particular kind of person to stand there and wait for the abuse to stop, and to come back again and again until the man will accept your help.

And the ghosts who end up in the Sunday School Publishing Board building are often still very traumatized. Some women cannot be approached by the male employee. Any help they get must come from the soft voice of another woman. Some men cannot come forward for a woman, cannot talk to a woman they don't know, even after all this time. Some want to stay and get even. Some cannot leave until they've relayed a message to a loved one.

"Those break my heart," my informant told me. "Who knows how long it's been since they've seen that other person? One hundred and sixty years? One hundred and seventy? And they don't even know that if they'd just be on their way they'd be reunited with that person. I am always so sorry they've wasted so much time, but praise Jesus that their suffering is about to be over."

"Do you really think that?" I asked.

"No," she said, "Certainly not in every case. But I will say this: when that was my job, one thing I learned is that I can't know what God's judgment will be. I have my opinions, of course. But I know God is merciful beyond understanding, so it's not my job to do anything more or less than fill my heart with compassion and then use that to help these folks get on to the next thing. I have faith I will see most of them again, and they won't be suffering, and they won't be scared, and they will be whole through Jesus. I couldn't have done it if I didn't know that's the truth."

"Do you think there will come a time when no one needs to do your job?" I asked.

"Yes, yes I do," she said. "We're needed less now than we were when I was working, and I was needed far less than my predecessor. But we're just one place in one city. I often wonder if anyone is doing this same work in other places. I hope so. I cannot bear to think otherwise."

October 30th

THE PURPLE IMPALA

Denny Wilcox was a police officer. He served with Metro for almost fifteen years. The end of his career started with a simple enough traffic stop—four Mexican kids in a twenty-year old Impala painted bright purple, rolling on rims that were weighted to stay still when the car moved, giving the illusion that the car was floating.

"They were obviously gang-bangers," Wilcox told me. "Covered in tattoos. I was giving them shit, all 'Hey, ese' just to see if it would get a rise out of them. The little one in the back seat said, 'You know, we speak English,' but the driver said, 'Let it go.'

"I didn't have a good reason, other than that they looked like trouble, to have pulled them over. And they didn't give me a good reason to keep them stopped. I wish to God either thing would have happened. Either make it so I never pulled them over, or give me a reason to keep them a little longer. But I let them go. They said, 'Thank you, officer,' and then, as I was watching them drive off, right when they crossed Thompson Lane ... and they had the green ... a car comes out of nowhere and just plows into them.

"You've got to know those Impalas are like tanks. Still, it was nothing but a pile of twisted metal and broken glass. I have seen my share of dead bodies, but I had never seen someone die right in front of me. And they all died— those four guys and the driver of the other car. We never did figure out why she didn't stop. Tox came back clean.

"I don't know.

"I went to tell their families. Guillermo Cortez? His mom fell to the ground when I told her. She didn't even make a noise. She just laid there like she was waiting for the earth to swallow her. His cousin Jose was the scrawny one in the

205

back. His girlfriend had just had a baby. When I showed up, she said, 'So, he's dead,' like she was just expecting it. 'Who did it?' and I told her it was just an accident. She looked at me like she couldn't make sense of what I was saying. 'How can that be?'

"Frankie Hernandez's family wouldn't even open the door for me. I knew they were home, but they wouldn't answer. I found someone three doors down who went and talked to them. They never did claim his body."

"Weird," I said.

"No, I get it," he said, "They were afraid to even be on our radar, afraid they'd be deported. And the fourth one was just called 'Sarge.' If he had a name, we never learned it. If there was someone to tell he was gone, I never found them. Of all of them, that was the worst. Someone out there must have given a shit about that kid, you know? And, as far as I know, they never knew what happened to him."

Wilcox was silent a long time. I'd come to expect that from folks. Men, especially, seemed to need long silences in order to get their stories out.

"Here's the thing." His voice startled both of us. "Four months later, I'm driving down Nolensville Road and I see a purple Impala, just like theirs. And it's raining, not hard, but still, and they don't have their headlights on. So I flash the car over and before I even get out of my car, I run the plates and they come back to Guillermo Cortez. I'm still thinking this has got to be the biggest motherfuck of a coincidence. But, hey, maybe there's a cousin and he's got himself a purple Impala in honor of his dead relative. So I get out of the car and I walk up to the window.

"And there is Guillermo Cortez. As real as you are. And he looks at me and he gives me a sly grin and he says, 'Officer Wilcox, you need a ride?' and Jose says, 'It's okay. We speak English.' and I can't even scream. I'm just standing there, my hands shaking and my mouth open, and as I'm watching them, not an arm's reach away from me, the car just fades from view. Like a fog lifting."

"Holy shit," I said.

"Well, you can bet that once my captain hears that I ran the plate of a dead kid, thinking I was pulling him over, I got a free trip to the shrink."

He paused again, to take a long drink of beer. "It happened again. Not just once. I saw that damn car all the time. I just never told anyone I was still seeing it. But one night, I said yes."

"Wait, what?"

"I pulled them over. Cortez asked me if I wanted a ride and I said yes. I got in the car with them."

"You got in the ghost car?"

Wilcox took another long swig off of his beer.

"I can't really explain it. You know how it is sometimes, late at night, when the traffic lights are all blinking yellow? How it feels like everyone in Nashville has vanished and it's just you and the useless traffic lights telling you to be careful, though there's nothing left to be careful about? How it feels like the whole empty city is yours?

"That's what it was like. They had cold beers. We all drank them. One of them had a bottle of tequila. We passed it around. After a while I could smell the odor of marijuana mixing in with the cigarette smoke, but I didn't care. They told stories about some guy they'd beat up or about some girl they saw who was so beautiful they couldn't stand it. And that big old purple Impala just floated over the city, slid in between cars, took turns down roads that haven't existed in years. And there were all these people, some living, most dead, just walking down the street or driving in their cars, a city of ghosts—a whole city of ghosts. Everywhere you looked. Ghosts right next to us, passing through us. Some trying to get our attention, some trying to ignore us.

"And we just drove by them, our windows down, our

music blaring. And those that turned to see us, they saw how beautiful we were, and we could see how beautiful they were.

"These guys, they saw everything. One or the other of them would notice just the most random shit. 'Oh, hey, watch the bounce in that guy's step.' 'Shit, have you ever seen a little kid that pissed?' or whatever. It was just you couldn't see enough.

"I said to them, 'I am so sorry,' and they just laughed. 'It's all good,' Sarge said. I know that sounds stupid, but it blew my mind then. It was like words were more, bigger, fuller. I don't know. Everything was just more beautiful. Seeing it from that car let you see that.

"Eventually, they dropped me off. Again, I said, 'I'm so sorry,' and Guillermo grabbed my arm and said, 'It's not important. Being sorry isn't important.' I patted the roof of their car and they drove off. I thought I had been gone for hours, but, when I got back in my car, only like ten minutes had passed.

"I quit right after that."

"Why?" I asked.

"I just couldn't stand what a goddamn waste people make of it all, you know?"

*October 31*st

THE DEVIL LIVES ON LEWIS STREET,
I SWEAR

We tell people that there are so many churches, so many denominational headquarters in town—from the Methodists to the Baptists—because we are literally the buckle of the Bible belt. This may be true, but doesn't it seem strange?

Why do we need a church every block and a half?

Or have you ever considered why it is that a road might need to change names three times, from, say Franklin Pike to Eighth Avenue to Rosa Parks Boulevard or from Harding to West End to Broadway, or from Murfreesboro to Lafayette to Eighth?

Why roads jut into each other at weird angles? Why you can get on an Old Hickory Boulevard anywhere in town, but you can't stay on the road to circle around the whole town?

Just who, exactly, is the town trying to keep lost?

You won't ever hear anyone come out and say it, but the truth is that folks are afraid of the Devil. Yes, the literal Devil.

Where to even start?

If we start now, it's like this—the Devil has the shoulders of a man who is used to working. And lately, he comes out on his front porch wearing nothing but a pair of shorts and a light sheen of sweat, with a beer in one hand, and most of the women on Lewis street (and some of the men) make excuses to walk by, to watch how his muscles move under his skin, to measure almost unconsciously the span of those shoulders with their hands.

A woman can rest a hand on each shoulder and put

her ear up against his chest, and still feel like there is room to spare. Maybe that's how come it's so easy for things to get out of hand—one woman, two women, three, four. Even before you get his clothes off, he seems large enough to take it.

But the story goes back. The Devil has lived here, on and off, for a long, long time.

Long before there even was a Nashville.

Back then, the gates of Hell were marked by twin elms. And if you passed between those elms after saying the right words, you would end up in the Devil's realm. And the rumor was that they were common words, nothing so tricky as "Open Sesame" or "Rumpelstiltskin." Just ordinary words. Two children might be running through the field and one would say to the other, "I'll race you to the two elms," and they would take off, and one would see something shiny in the grass between the trees and he would turn to his companion and say "Look here."

And he would be gone.

For hundreds of years, people avoided the area. The trees were eventually chopped down. And cemeteries were put up where the trees had stood, as both an acknowledgment and an attempt to mitigate, to have the help of the godly dead to keep the gate sealed.

Almost no one believes it works.

They say the Devil's front door is still just a couple of hundred feet off of Elm Hill Pike.

And that, they say, is how Elizabeth Bennett came to know him.

No one knows much about Bennett's life before 1786. Not for sure who her people were. Not what she did to get by. Bennett is a Choctaw name, in that screwed-up Southern way, but folks claimed she was from North Carolina, which would seem to suggest she was Cherokee.

210

I was told that she was taken from her family when she was quite young, twelve or thirteen, and married to a man named Bennett; that she had been a Hensley before that.

Mr. Bennett had not gotten even a mile from her parents' home before he threw her on the ground and jammed his knee between her legs so hard she almost forgot to breathe. He pressed his hand against the side of her face and left, on one side, the red shadows of his fingers. On the other side, for an hour, you could make out the outline of the plants her face had been pressed into.

"So," she thought as he went at her, "this is what it means to be a woman."

He took her to live on the banks of the Cumberland among people he thought would leave them alone, not far from where she would enter Nashville history. She was uniformly well-liked, but though everyone knew Bennett was mistreating her, no one confronted him, because they were not her people.

One day a woman squatted next to her creek-side and asked her if she had heard of the legend of the twin elms. Of course she had not.

"Just send him there, as often as you can, and he may vanish. People who go there vanish."

And so Elizabeth went there. She fished near there. She trapped near there. She collected roots and herbs and leaves near there. She walked around there for no reason. And she never disappeared.

Most likely because she never had anyone with her to say "Oh, look here," to even if she had anything interesting to look at.

But one day, she found the Devil. He was lying half in the creek, at the end of where Lewis Street is now, and he was badly injured. She recognized him immediately. As much by the smell of sulfur as anything.

She rolled him out of the water, lifted his head onto her lap, and brushed his hair out of his face.

"What can I do for you?" she asked.

"What would you do for me?" he whispered hoarsely.

"I'm making no deals with you, my friend," she said, grinning in spite of herself. "I'm asking you an honest question. I don't know how to help you, but if you tell me, I will do my best."

"Will you make a fire?"

"I will make you a fire." And she did.

"Now roll me in it."

"Are you sure?"

"Of course."

She paused just a second. "May I say something?"

"Please."

"You're not nearly as unpleasant as I thought you'd be."

"I'm actually rarely unpleasant," he said, grinning wickedly.

Some will tell you that it was later, when Mr. Bennett was visiting the sulfur springs by the salt lick and was bitten by a large, black dog and got what appeared to be an extremely painful case of rabies and died, that Elizabeth Bennett's life changed.

But I believe it was that grin that did it.

She rolled him into the fire and there was a noise like bacon in a skillet and he vanished into thin air.

When he came to her, after she was officially a widow, he said, "I will repay your kindness."

"How so?" she asked.

"You are free."

"I don't know what that means," she told him.

"You can have whatever you want."

Possibly, he assumed she would want to be Queen of America or to return to her parents or... who knows?

"I want you to stay for dinner," she said. And he did.

By candlelight, she traced the line of his shoulders with her finger. She brushed his long hair out of his face. She looked into his black eyes. And she kissed him. She did it. She led him.

He's clever that way.

"What can I call you?" she asked.

"I've always been partial to Joseph," he said."I could be Joseph Durand for a while."

When he left, she said, "I'll wait for you."

"Why?"

"Are you not coming back?" She asked. He cocked his head and looked at her.

"Of course."

"Then I..."

"You are free to do what you want."

And so she did.

When the Frenchman, Timothy Demonbreun arrived, she was like no one he'd ever met. She hunted, she trapped, she cussed and drank, and sat with the men when it suited her and sat with the women when it suited her. She let Demonbreun cook her dinner, and when it was done she burped in appreciation.

It was, quite possibly, the least surprising thing to happen in the short history of Nashville when she was brought up on charges for having Timothy's bastard child in 1787. They took up together, in a cave near the two elms, some say so that she could watch for Durand.

There was a lot of anticipation in the community about Durand's return. Not that most folks knew he was the Devil, but even now, when a woman takes up with another man while hers is away, people are curious about what's going to happen.

What happened was that when Durand returned, Durand and Demonbreun went out and chopped down the biggest tree they could find and fashioned a large bed for Elizabeth. The three of them shared it. And then Durand and Elizabeth got married.

And they continued to share it.

Eventually word got around about Durand, about how you shouldn't play cards against him if you wanted to keep your money, about how his just being in a room could lead men to fist-fighting, about how babies whose fat cheeks he pinched would stop eating.

There were rumors that he could dry up a cow just by looking at it and that he was always followed by three black crows. I don't know how true those stories were, but I know folks were afraid of him.

But people were more terrified of Elizabeth. Elizabeth would chase a man from his home at the wrong end of his own rifle if she learned that he beat his wife. Elizabeth would sit in the back of the church and ask when a woman could be preacher. Elizabeth would vote in every election, just for the satisfaction of making them take her ballot, even knowing they would just tear it up once she left.

Durand would often smile and say to her, "You may, quite possibly, cause more trouble than I ever could."

And she would laugh and say, "I doubt that."

She lived almost a century, but as women often do, she eventually died, out on her farm halfway to Ashland

City.

The Devil was heartbroken. Inconsolable.

Elizabeth's youngest son twice had to ride into Nashville and make his way through crowded inns and taverns until he discovered where the old man was slumped over a table. The young man would brush his hair out of his face, whisper, "Let's get you home," and take him back out to the farm, where he could sober up and rest.

Years have gone by, and still the Devil comes to Nashville. Some say that he comes with her and some say that he comes looking for her.

I don't know which is true. But I know better than to play cards with a man who smells slightly of sulfur, and to take any story he tells you with a grain of salt.

Acknowledgements

Thanks to Nina Melechen, Barry Mazor, Samantha Yeargin, Beth Downey, Chris Wage, Kristin Whittlesey, Mary Mancini, and Bart Phillips. Thanks to everyone who read the stories and provided feedback and special thanks to everyone who then shared their own ghost stories.

About the Author

Betsy Phillips lives just outside of Nashville in Whites Creek, TN. She has actually seen a ghost in her back yard.

Her website is tinycatpants.com.

Made in the USA
San Bernardino, CA
01 August 2014